A Glimpse
of Paradise

A Glimpse
of Paradise

Cathie Linz

Five Star
Unity, Maine

Five Star Romance Series.

Published in 2001 in conjunction with Cathie Linz.

Set in 11 pt. Plantin by Al Chase.

Printed in the United States on permanent paper.

Library of Congress Cataloging-in-Publication Data

Linz, Cathie.
    A glimpse of paradise / Cathie Linz.
      p.   cm.
    ISBN 0-7862-3119-X (hardcover : alk. paper)
    1. Women psychologists — Fiction. 2. Television
journalists — Fiction. 3. Women's shelters — Fiction.
I. Title.
PS3562.I558 G57 2001
  813'.54—dc21   00-052835

A Glimpse

of Paradise

PROLOGUE

Thursday, May 9, 11:23 P.M. (EST)

"I've had it!" Marnie Lathrope exclaimed in disgust. Smacking the off button on her color television set, she sent the image on the screen shrinking into a black hole. "Who does Logan McCallister think he is? God?" She completed two turns around her spacious living room before continuing her tirade. "You know, Elaine, I'm not the type who gets angry for no reason."

Elaine Casper nodded understandingly and continued nibbling on a guacamole-laden taco chip.

The nod was all the encouragement Marnie needed. "But this is too much. Can you imagine McCallister calling our plans for opening a shelter 'a Band-Aid solution'?" Marnie restlessly shoved aside a loose curl of her auburn hair, her brown eyes flashing. "And how about his insinuations that we're wasting the citizens of South Carolina's tax dollars?" Her compact breasts positively heaved beneath her blue T-shirt as she righteously voiced the demand "Whatever happened to objective reporting?"

"The concept was probably canceled because there was a lack of viewer interest," Elaine replied, having finished the last of the taco chips.

"God knows we had enough trouble receiving that state money," said Marnie as she resumed her pacing. "We don't need any moralizing from some sensation-seeking glitzy reporter by the name of Logan McCallister."

"Hear! Hear!" Elaine applauded. "Let's tar 'n' feather him 'n' run him out of town," she drawled.

Marnie laughed at her friend's exaggerated look of fiendish anticipation. "Sounds good, but I don't think it would help our image any."

Elaine's expression became thoughtful. "There may be something you can do that would help our image."

Marnie stopped her pacing. "What?"

"I happen to know that McCallister will be speaking at a banquet next month. Here"—Elaine held out an empty bowl—"get us some more taco chips, and we'll plan our strategy for getting even."

CHAPTER ONE

Sunday, June 16, 8:32 P.M. (EST)

"Did I miss much?" The formally dressed man who dropped into the empty seat beside Marnie did not speak with a southern drawl, which set him apart from the other occupants of the Charleston banquet hall that evening.

"You're late." Marnie's reprimand was coolly delivered. She'd been worried that, after all her planning, Logan McCallister wasn't going to show up. But here he was, finally. An hour late!

"I would have been here sooner had I known *you* were waiting for me." The teasing words fell from his lips with practiced ease—clearly Logan was accustomed to handling women. Yet something special about this particular woman caught his attention, and held it.

Marnie, too, felt the incredibly strong, and surprisingly sudden, tug of attraction. Logan's televised image had been deceptive, for it had given no hint of the sheer dynamic personality of the man.

His masculine curiosity aroused, Logan bestowed a blatantly intimate look upon her—a look that began at the top of her head of gorgeous red hair, traveled across her flushed face, and drifted over her sexy body in a very expressive appraisal. The masculine gleam in his eyes reflected his approval. His gaze slid over the silk of her moss-green dress, noting the way the material clung to her curves. The finer stylistic details of the garment, such as the flange shoulders and jacquard print, may have escaped his notice, but little else did.

9

"Have you been waiting long?" His inflection could only be labeled seductive.

Marnie's "Yes" was unintentionally breathy. *Five weeks and four days to be exact,* she silently continued. Ever since that fateful night when she and Elaine had sat over a fresh bowl of taco chips and concocted tonight's scenario.

It had seemed so simple then. Debating Logan McCallister on the influence of television news on society had sounded right up Marnie's alley. Here was her chance to get even, to issue a verbal condemnation as bitingly disparaging as his news reports. But now that the moment had arrived, Marnie was beginning to have second thoughts.

The reason for her hesitancy: Logan McCallister. That look he'd given her had positively scorched all her icy defenses with the effectiveness of a blow torch! He had to be the most magnetically appealing man she'd ever come into contact with. And here she was, with him sitting next to her.

"Has anyone ever called you Red?" he inquired.

"No one who lived to tell the tale. No," Marnie shot back. What was wrong with her? She was twenty-seven, a professional woman who'd met plenty of men more attractive than Logan.

Logan's appreciative laughter rang out between them. His mirth gave Marnie the opportunity to do a brief study of his appearance, and her scrutiny, intended to be impersonal, wound up getting quite personal indeed. The strength of Logan's attractive features lent him a slightly rakish air, an image reinforced by the unruliness of the dark curly hair that brushed against the collar of his understated suit. The lines around his eyes and mouth spoke of a man who laughed often, while the width of his shoulders and the leanness of his waist indicated a man who kept himself in shape. At a guess, she'd say he was in his early to mid thirties. That air of casual self-confidence he possessed must have taken at least that long to acquire!

Aware of her interest, Logan said, "Hope you like what you see, Red." His lips lifted in a devilish grin. "You here alone?"

Although embarrassed at being caught staring, Marnie still managed a mocking reply: "No, there are approximately three hundred other people in this room with me."

"Funny." He sighed theatrically and then softly sang, *"I only have eyes for you."*

"Perhaps you need glasses," she observed dryly.

"Only for reading."

Marnie was surprised to hear a faint note of defensiveness in his voice. Vulnerability of any kind was not an element of the mental picture she'd originally painted of Logan McCallister. But then, neither was this feeling of physical attraction she was experiencing. *Goes to show how inaccurate mental pictures can be.* Her impression of him was undergoing a rapid overhaul, and she found the new image to be infinitely more disturbing than the glitzy original. Intent on changing the subject, she found herself asking, "So, are you ready for your speech this evening?"

"Sure am. Let's see." Logan pulled several index cards from the inside pocket of his jacket. "The topic is 'The Influence of Television News on Society.' Pretty heavy stuff." Tossing her a conspiratorial grin, he said in an undertone, "I understand the other side's even brought in a psychologist."

"So I've heard."

Marnie's smile prompted Logan to indulge in a guessing game. "I'll bet that tall, distinguished-looking guy over there is the shrink."

Marnie shook her head. "That's Dave Mileson. He sells life insurance."

11

"How about the portly man next to him?"

"John Dickerman, a dentist."

"A dentist, huh? At least I'm getting closer, which means my next guess will be the right one. The tall man with the mustache?"

Marnie was finding it difficult to control her laughter. This was better than she could have hoped for.

"Wrong man?" Logan asked.

"Wrong sex," Marnie answered in a half-choked voice.

"The shrink's a woman?"

Marnie nodded.

Meanwhile the master of ceremonies had approached the podium to begin his introductions for the speakers. "Ladies and gentlemen, we're very pleased to have Logan McCallister here with us tonight. Logan's series on arson is just one of the many investigative reports he's presented on the eleven-o'clock news. I'm sure you'll join me in welcoming him."

Logan courteously stood to accept the applause given him. The moment he resumed his seat, he resumed his guessing game. Leaning closer to Marnie he whispered, "I've got it! The beady-eyed woman at the next table?"

"No," Marnie whispered back. "The tall redhead sitting next to you."

Logan did a classic double take.

The master of ceremonies' second introduction came as if on cue. "And our other speaker this evening is Dr. Marnie Lathrope, a psychologist who'll share her views on the psychological effects of television news on its viewers."

Now Marnie stood to accept the applause.

"Was the dinner fillet of sole, by any chance?" Logan asked her once she had gracefully sat down again.

"No, roast beef." Her answer was spoken in a half whisper as the master of ceremonies launched into a brief discourse on the topic of the news media. "Why do you ask?"

"Because I'm experiencing a funny aftertaste of shoe leather." Logan plucked an imaginary tack from his lips. "Must be from the foot I've stuck in my mouth." He waited until she laughed, before voicing his grumbling accusation. "You could've told me."

"What!" Amusement lit her face. "And miss out on your entertaining search for the shrink?"

"You look too good to be a shrink."

The comment was one Marnie had heard many times before—heard and resented. She'd worked hard and long for her advanced degree. "Is that meant to be a compliment?" Her cool inflection informed him that she wasn't taking it as one.

"I'd love to sit here and ply you with compliments, Red, but—"

The amplified announcement now interrupted: "So without further ado, we'll get on with our first speaker, Logan McCallister."

"—I'm afraid I've got a speech to give," Logan murmured.

"Good luck," Marnie drawled.

Only after muttering "Why do I get the impression you've silently added 'you'll need it'?" did he stride up to the lecture podium.

"My job is to be your eyes and ears." Logan caught the audience's attention with that opening statement and held it throughout his speech. He was a natural speaker. His presentation was clear and concise as he enumerated the cases where the television as a news medium had had a positive impact on society.

Watching Logan as he spoke, Marnie knew she had a hard act to follow. It didn't take long for her attention to become as concentrated on the man as on his words. Logan

13

McCallister's brand of charm was dangerously powerful. The symptoms of physical attraction were not unknown to her, but this deep-seated recognition was new and disconcerting. Logan bore no resemblance to anyone she knew, so why this inner click when she looked at him?

Part of her mind continued its attempt to rationalize her feelings, while the other part concentrated on Logan. The end result was that Marnie had little time to become nervous about her own upcoming speech. Now that Logan had reached the end of his presentation, she joined in the applause, coolly ignoring the knowing look he sent her.

The master of ceremonies came forward once again to introduce Marnie. Then he joined Logan, who had already taken one of the seats to the side of the podium.

Marnie set her notebook on the wooden podium, efficiently adjusted the microphone to accommodate her height, and began speaking. "Mr. McCallister has pointed out what's right with television news. Now it is my turn to point out what's wrong."

She paused a moment to establish eye contact with several members of her audience. "The trend I find most alarming is the increasing depiction of bloodshed and violence on both the local and network newscasts. In the quest for higher ratings television viewers are being bombarded with images that are meant to grab their attention. These images are often brutal and gruesome.

"A case in point is the explicit shots of the bloodied bodies of victims of war or natural disasters that are indifferently flashed across the screen during a forty-two-second news brief. When one considers that these news briefs are often inserted between family-oriented TV shows that children may be watching, the inappropriateness of such programming is even more evident. There are other ways of covering the news

14

—ways that are more responsible and less theatrical."

The audience applauded heartily at that point, and at several others during the course of her speech.

Afterward the audience was given the opportunity to direct questions to either Marnie or Logan.

John Dickerman, the dentist that Logan had suggested might be the "shrink," stood to pose the first question. "Mr. McCallister, isn't it true that the press scrutinizes every institution except itself? A corrupt corporate executive or elected official can be fired or booted out of office, but what retribution does a broadcaster face?"

Logan joined Marnie at the podium to answer the question. "A broadcaster faces the same retribution as anyone else. We, too, can be fired if people find that what we're reporting is inaccurate or unfair. In fact, on a local level, broadcasters have been fired for much less. Something as intangible as loss of audience appeal can get you fired. In extreme cases things as trivial as a hairstyle or a low galvanic skin response have been cause for removal. In case you're unfamiliar with the technique," Logan went on to explain, "galvanic skin response, or GSR as it's called, is measured by placing electrodes on viewers' skin to record changes in the electrical impulses that the skin emits. In this way it can be determined whether the viewers were positively or negatively moved by the anchorpeople they were shown on a videotape."

Marnie had become familiar with GSR in the course of her own graduate work. She could only be grateful that no one was recording *her* GSR as she stood so close beside Logan. She had no doubt the results would indicate she was very positively moved by this particular broadcaster!

Once they'd finished answering questions from the audience and were back at their table, Logan congratulated

Marnie on her speech. "You're quite a formidable opponent, Red."

Formidable opponent. Funny he should put it that way. "So I've been told." A slight smile accompanied the wry acknowledgment.

"Oh?" Logan raised an inquiring brow. "By whom?"

"My grade-school principal."

His forehead furrowed in confusion. "I don't get it."

"As a child I had something of a quick temper," she heard herself explaining easily. "My parents used to tease me by claiming that they had twice as much trouble with me fighting in the grade-school playground as they did with my older brother, Ben. Consequently, I spent more than my fair share of time in the principal's office." After relating the childhood anecdote, Marnie immediately questioned her expansiveness. She wasn't in the habit of reminiscing about her childhood with strangers, regardless of how attractive they were. Why had she made an exception with Logan?

"A temper? You, Red?" Logan was shaking his head in mock disbelief. "I find that hard to believe."

"Keep calling me Red and I can guarantee you'll see a firsthand display of my temper," she warned him, the glint in her brown eyes putting him on official notice.

"Threats, Red?" Again he shook his head, tumbling several dark strands of hair onto his forehead. His eyes gleamed with humor as he chastised her: "I'm shocked that a doctor would use such methods."

"Local shrink threatens violence! Details at eleven!" Marnie mimicked the sensationalizing inflections of TV newscasters.

"You're pretty good at that." He congratulated her. "But anything you say to me is strictly off-the-record."

The journalistic term reminded her of Logan's unfavorable commentary on the shelter, and her thoughts switched to professional issues, away from personal ones. "I'd prefer that what we discuss remain on-the-record."

"That's a switch." Logan shrugged. "But if you insist." His grin should have warned her. "For the record, you've got gorgeous hair—it reminds me of the color of a newly minted penny."

"For the record, I resented your lightweight, mocking commentary on the prospective opening of a shelter for battered women," she crisply retorted, deciding to direct his attention away from her looks, to the importance of what she had to say.

Logan looked over his shoulder as if watching the departure of a fastball. Returning his confused gaze to her, he murmured, "That came out of left field."

"So did your commentary. 'A Band-Aid solution' is the way I believe you put it."

"I take it you're involved in this shelter?"

"How perceptive of you."

"Mmm." Logan didn't appear to be unduly put out by her antagonism as he thoughtfully stroked his index finger along his jaw. "And would this shelter have anything to do with your appearance here tonight?"

"It has everything to do with it."

"And here I was, hoping it was my magnetic charm." He heaved a soulful sigh and leaned back in his chair. His casual attitude, however, was belied by his line of questioning, which was blunt and direct. "May I ask why you didn't bring up this matter earlier? In your speech, for example?"

"I didn't think it would serve any purpose to drag specific charges into my presentation. My speech would be more effective if I presented universal complaints."

"I see. So your reason for being here tonight is strictly professional, correct?"

"Absolutely correct."

"Too bad. Because my interest in you is personal, not professional."

Marnie's brown eyes narrowed at his audacity. "No doubt you're planning an exposé on psychologists," she said sarcastically.

"Depends what you plan on exposing," he retorted with a raised brow and a look of masculine interest.

"Nothing!" she shot back, cursing the translucency of her skin, which now revealed a slight blush. She raised her hand automatically to her cheek in an attempt to shield its redness from view.

Logan leaned closer to study her face. "You're not—"

"No, I'm not!" Marnie hurriedly denied, certain he was going to accuse her of blushing.

"—busy tomorrow night, are you?" he went on to say deliberately. Grinning at her apparent discomfiture, he ran a finger across the knuckles of the hand she'd lowered from her cheek to the table. "Caught ya!" Despite his triumphant words, he made no attempt to hold her hand. Instead he continued his alluring exploration of the back of her fingers.

"That wasn't the question I was expecting you to ask," she tried explaining.

"It's the question you answered, and I intend holding you to it." Now his fingers loosely enfolded hers.

In other circumstances Marnie might have found the clasp to be restrictive, but with Logan she experienced a *frisson,* as if her skin, too, recognized his touch.

"If we could get back to the matter at hand," she requested in an aloof voice.

Her attempts to slip her fingers away from his were

thwarted by Logan as he lifted their clasped hands. "Sure. The matter at hand?" His thumb stroked its way across the sensitive skin between her thumb and index finger. "How about, you feel as good as you look?"

"I was talking about the shelter for battered women."

"I wasn't."

"I know." This time Marnie was able to free her hand, although it was with the disturbing knowledge that Logan was humoring her by allowing her to do so. "I'm serious." She threw him an indignant look.

"So am I." His bold gaze touched her as tangibly as his hands had.

"Not about the same thing." She gathered up her small clutch purse. "I can see it's useless trying to speak to you about this." Briskly shoving back her chair, she rose to her feet. If Logan had no intention of listening to her, there were other people present tonight who might be able to help support the shelter.

"Wait!" Logan's fingers automatically shot out to manacle her wrist. "Where are you going?"

"Since you won't discuss the subject seriously, I'll find someone else who will," she stated bluntly.

"Sit down." Logan gently tugged her back into her seat. "We'll talk about this shelter of yours." He waited until she'd relaxed before softly adding, "But only so that we can get that out of the way and proceed to more important subjects."

"I happen to feel that the subject of battered women is a very important one, Mr. McCallister." Now it was Marnie's turn to pin him with an uncompromisingly direct look. "Are you aware that in any one year nearly six million women are abused by their husbands or boyfriends?"

"Actually I was aware of that," he said, much to her surprise. "I did a segment on family violence, which is when I

19

made the comment you seem to have taken such exception to. Wouldn't you agree that one shelter for battered women in a city of over three hundred thousand inhabitants is indeed a mere Band-Aid affixed to a growing social problem?"

"It's better than nothing," she shot back. "Do you have any idea how much work it took to raise enough money from the state and from private foundations to fund this shelter?"

Logan shook his head, his eyes fixed by the vibrant concern displayed on her features. Marnie obviously had a wealth of fire in her, and he wanted her to glow like this for him.

Unaware of the intimate direction of Logan's thoughts, Marnie answered her own question. "It's taken us three years to get this far, and the shelter still hasn't opened." Frustrated because he still made no reply, she tacked on one last blistering statement: "After all of our efforts we don't need some slick TV entertainer sabotaging things!"

"Your grade-school principal was right, Red. You do pack a powerful punch!" Logan shook his head in rueful amusement. "TV entertainer, hmmm?" Reaching into his jacket pocket, he removed a pack of cigarettes. His eyes and voice were equally mocking as he asked, "Is a condemned man allowed one last smoke?"

"I'm allergic to cigarette smoke, so if you want to light up, I'm afraid you'll have to go to another table. This table is for nonsmokers." Marnie's southern accent softened the words, which she'd intended to be abrupt. She was not accustomed to being laughed at.

Logan responded by clenching his fingers around the pack of cigarettes. "If you're allergic to cigarette smoke, then I'll just have to give up smoking." He tossed the now badly crumpled cellophane-wrapped pack into the table's pristine ashtray.

She looked at him in amazement. "Just like that?"

"Just like that," he said.

"How long have you been a smoker?"

"Off and on for about five years now."

"It may not be that easy to quit," she warned him.

"Thanks." Logan gave a wry grimace. "I really needed to hear that."

Marnie relented. "I'm sorry, I don't mean to discourage you."

"How reassuring." His husky words were accompanied by a sidelong glance so potent that she could actually feel it searing through her.

You're a psychologist—she sternly sought to calm her racing heart. *You're supposed to be able to effectively deal with people. So deal with him!* But before she could do so, Logan spoke again.

"Despite your obvious thoughts to the contrary, the news media can have a very positive effect. Amid all the razzmatazz, TV journalists do manage to accomplish some good."

"I don't deny that the news media could have a positive effect," she replied, glad that they'd returned to the original subject of their discussion. "However, the fact remains that in an overwhelming number of cases they don't. The chase for higher ratings is what directs station policies, not a noble quest for the truth."

"Television broadcasting is a business, just as psychology is a business."

She took exception to this. "Psychology is not a business, it's a profession."

"So it's a professional business." Logan shrugged, unconvinced. "Shrinks still have a reputation for raking in profits from other people's pain."

"And television broadcasters have a reputation for being more concerned with the shape of their mouths than what comes out of them," a furious Marnie shot back.

To her surprise Logan agreed with her. "Granted. The point I'm making is that neither accusation fits either one of *us.*" The words were said with a direct honesty that disarmed her. "So wouldn't it be best if we dispensed with all these preconceived ideas and simply got to know each other better?"

Marnie found it impossible to break off the magnetic eye contact he'd established. Her emotions were on a roller coaster with this man. One minute she was furious with him, the next entranced. For a woman who made a living out of analyzing human behavior, it was disconcerting, to say the least, to find her own behavior so volatile!

Logan had perfected visual communication to an art form that was downright sinful. Even now, his eyes were courting her with unspoken words and intimate promises. Caught up in the spell, Marnie realized that Logan's eyes weren't dark brown, like her own. Instead the irises were actually the color of a fine sherry flecked with amber. And around the perimeter was a ring of burnt umber.

What had they been talking about? She couldn't remember. Something about getting to know each other. Marnie tore her gaze from his and collected her scattered thoughts. "I gather from your accent that you're not originally from Charleston?"

"In the first place, I don't have an accent, you do. And a very sexy accent it is, too," Logan added with a slow smile that accelerated her already rapid pulse. "As for your question, I grew up in Montana."

"Montana's a long way from South Carolina. What brought you here?"

"A 1977 Datsun 280Z," he replied with a perfectly straight face.

A knowing smile lifted the corners of her lips. "I see." So

the man didn't like talking about his past. Interesting.

"Probably more than you're meant to," he muttered to himself, somewhat disconcerted by the indulgent look she'd sent him.

"What?" She hadn't quite heard what he'd said.

"Nothing. How about you?"

Following his lead, Marnie answered, "I came in a 1984 Chrysler."

"Came from where?"

"From home."

"Which is?"

"In Charleston."

"That narrows it down tremendously," he said mockingly, impatiently drumming his fingers against the white table-cloth. "Why are you afraid to tell me where you live?"

"What makes you think I'm afraid?"

"Why do you answer a question with a question?"

"Why do you?"

"A reporter is trained to ask questions. What's your excuse?"

"Same as yours. A psychologist is also trained to ask questions."

"Sounds like we've already got a lot in common," he said.

"You think so?" Marnie's inflection relayed her own skepticism.

"Definitely. Now, about tomorrow. Where would you like to go for dinner?"

"Mr. McCallister, I really don't think—"

"Logan."

Intent as she was on delivering her speech, she blinked at his unexpected interruption. "What?"

"My name is Logan. My tax accountant is the only one who calls me Mr. McCallister."

"Logan, then." She used his first name with marked reluctance.

"Umm, before you go on, I feel it only fair to warn you that I don't handle rejection very well." Balancing his chin between thumb and index finger—à la Jack Benny—he gave her a slanting, delightfully doleful look. "Being a psychologist yourself, I'm sure you wouldn't want to do anything that would further bruise my self-image."

"At a guess, I'd say your self-image is robustly healthy."

"Is that your professional diagnosis?" He leaned close to ask the question, his lips a few inches from her cheek.

The woman beneath the psychologist's cool exterior reacted to the intimacy of Logan's voice, the tangy scent of his after-shave, the warmth of his presence. "Consider it a personal observation," she huskily replied. One of many personal observations she'd made about Logan McCallister, most of which were infinitely more personal—bordering as they did on the downright erotic!

It was a quest for knowledge that had first sent Marnie onto the academic path leading to a PhD in clinical psychology. That same quest for knowledge was now leading her down a path of quite another sort. Perhaps she would do well to investigate this physical phenomenon she was experiencing. It was certainly unlike anything she'd experienced before.

While Marnie was in the midst of her self-interrogation, Logan put his own interpretation on her silence. "One of my personal observations about *you* is that you seem to be avoiding my invitation. I meant what I said earlier. I won't take no for an answer. So you can just forget that polite refusal you're no doubt composing. . . ."

Take risks. Isn't that what she advised her patients? Living involved a series of taking risks, right? She nodded decisively, her mind made up. "Yes."

Logan halted in midsentence. "Yes?"

"I hate to contradict such an illustrious communicator," she drawled with gentle mockery. "But the truth is, I was composing an acceptance, not a refusal. Simply put, my answer is yes. I'd like to go out with you, Logan."

CHAPTER TWO

Logan quickly recovered from his surprise. Dr. Marnie Lathrope, he was learning, rarely reacted the way he expected her to. No doubt, that was one reason why she intrigued him so. That, and the fact that she was a stunning redhead with a figure that made him feel like an oversexed teenage boy! "Fine. I'll pick you up tomorrow night at seven. Where do you live?"

Marnie adroitly parried his question by saying, "It would be easier for me if we could meet at a restaurant."

Logan saw through her polite ploy. "Don't you trust me?"

"Sorry, it's a personal policy of mine."

"What is?" The mocking tilt of his head matched the questioning angle of his right eyebrow. "Not trusting me?"

"No, not giving out my address to anyone I barely know."

"I'd love to know you—barely." That last word, huskily spoken, was an invitation.

Eyeing his broad shoulders and trim physique in discreet speculation, Marnie privately confessed to a similar desire. Yet she had the strangest feeling that she already knew the splendors of Logan's body; that her fingers had once coasted across his bare skin, her lips had once tasted. . . . She applied an abrupt brake to her wayward thoughts. *This is no place for a sexual fantasy, Marnie,* she silently berated herself. *You're in the middle of a conversation here.* "Have you heard of the Sweet Pepper?"

Logan blinked, as if he, too, had been caught up in a web of erotic thought. "Sweet Pepper?"

"It's a restaurant here in Charleston."

26

"Right." He nodded as if clearing his head. "I've heard of it."

"Then I'll meet you there tomorrow night at seven."

"Excuse me, Mr. McCallister?" The beady-eyed woman from the next table, one of the people Logan had mistakenly guessed to be the shrink, came barreling over to him. "My daughter, Priscilla, is interested in a career in broadcasting, and I wonder if you might give me some pointers to pass along to her?" She boldly commandeered one of the vacant chairs at the table and sat down.

Marnie couldn't resist saying, "Call him Logan. Only his tax accountant calls him Mr. McCallister."

Leaving Logan in the unidentified woman's more than eager hands was a low trick, but Marnie knew this was her one chance to make an unimpeded departure. She'd seen the arguments already forming in Logan's eyes right before they'd been interrupted. So Marnie seized the opportunity to make her escape. "I really must be going. I've got an early day tomorrow. Good night." Marnie's farewell was directed to both a glowering Logan and a glowing what's-her-name.

"I'll see you tomorrow night at seven," Logan rejoined, his eyes adding the clear message that he would exact his pound of flesh from her then.

During the drive back to her Battery-side condominium, Marnie had time to ponder her powerful response to Logan. However, after having narrowly avoided a reckless driver, Marnie resolved to shelve the self-analysis until she was safely at home —preferably in the security of her own bed!

But the four-poster canopied bed with its flower-sprigged linens proved to be a veritable hotbed of unrest. Far from providing the relative peace she sought, the antique double bed brought to mind the unbidden image of a warm male to share it with. Had Marnie been a parapsychologist, she might

well have been tempted to accuse Logan of spiritual possession of her soul, so firmly had he lodged himself in her
thoughts! As it was, she was forced to sip at a glass of white
wine and immerse herself in the latest issue of *Psychology
Today* before she was able to turn off the Tiffany-style bedside lamp and go to sleep.

"How was the great debate last night?" Marnie was asked
the moment she stepped into her office the next morning.

The question came from Diane, the extroverted recep-
tionist/office manager who practically ran the group practice
with which Marnie was associated. Officially the group practice was headed by a medical doctor, a talented psychiatrist
by the name of Dr. Chapman. But when Dr. Chapman
needed to find a lost file, or locate a patient's medical history,
he came to Diane, as did the four psychologists who worked
with Dr. Chapman. Marnie was no exception to the rule.
However, today the shoe was on the other foot. Diane was
waiting for information from her.

Knowing she was only delaying the inevitable, Marnie answered Diane's question with one of her own. "Good morning,
Diane. How's the schefflera doing today?" The receptionist's
green thumb had turned their waiting room into a restful, verdant oasis. "Has its case of spider mites cleared up?"

Diane sent her a chastising smile. "Come on, Dr.
Lathrope, I can smell an avoidance tactic a mile off."

Marnie slipped off her buttercup-yellow suit jacket and
laughed softly. "You've been working here too long."

"Well, there's always the chance that that neurologist on
the second floor will come whisk me away to work for him,"
Diane murmured in a semipensive tone.

"He'd better not dare." Marnie threw her hands out in
surrender. "All right, Diane. The debate went very well last
night."

"I'm glad." Diane dropped down into the comfortable chair normally reserved for Marnie's patients, and scooted it right up to the desk. Leaning forward, elbows propped a few centimeters from Marnie's brass nameplate, she said, "So tell me. Is Logan McCallister as good-looking as he seems on TV?"

"I never knew you thought Logan was good-looking." Marnie looked at the thirty-three-year-old Diane in surprise. "I thought you preferred the anchorman—what's his name?—Bill Singleton."

"Not anymore. Oh, I admit Bill Singleton is better-looking in a smooth sort of way, but Logan's got a certain something that's infinitely more appealing. There's something wild and untamed about Logan. He's his own man, not some network ninny. So tell me, is he as sexy offscreen as on?"

Marnie was none too pleased at Diane's glowing accolades. Consequently her own reply was rather brief, although grudgingly honest. "Yes, he is."

"Thanks, that's all I wanted to know. And now that I do, I'll get back to work." Diane jumped out of the chair, neatly returning it to its usual position across from Marnie's desk. "Amy Pektin's here for her nine-thirty appointment."

Marnie checked the digital readout of her desktop clock: 9:20. "She's only ten minutes early today!"

"I know. She's making real headway. I'll spend the next ten minutes telling her so and then send her in."

"Thanks, Diane."

One of Amy Pektin's problems was a fear of being late. Marnie was making progress with her, though. When Amy had first come in to see Marnie, she'd been half an hour early. Now it was down to ten minutes, and that was real progress.

Marnie's great capacity for empathy made her very popular with her patients. She had a heavy caseload. Most of the people she saw in the course of her practice had problems coping with one or more aspects of their lives. Marnie helped them deal with their individual situations by talking about the choices they had. Too many times she'd seen people back themselves into a corner and become panicked because they couldn't see any way out.

With Amy Pektin, Marnie had used a goal-oriented approach. First they went over the worst possible thing that could happen to Amy if she was late. Then they dissected each fear as it arose. The next steps involved homework assignments of a type. Something as seemingly easy as going for an hour without looking at a clock was difficult for a patient with a fixation about time. Thankfully, Marnie's approach was working with Amy.

A majority of Marnie's patients were women—not because women had more difficulty coping, but because they had a greater willingness to seek help. One of her few male patients was Mr. Hooper, whose self-image had taken a serious beating when his wife of eighteen years left him. After her eleven-thirty appointment with Mr. Hooper, Marnie had penciled in a lunch date with her friend and fellow psychologist Elaine Casper, the instigator of last night's debate.

But it wasn't meant to be. Elaine buzzed Marnie from her office just down the hall at twelve thirty with the upsetting news that a child Elaine had been treating had been admitted into the hospital for an appendectomy and was panicking. Elaine was the group practice's specialist in child psychology. The distraught parents had requested Elaine's assistance in calming the child's fears.

"That's all right, Elaine. We'll talk tomorrow." *That will give me more time to come up with an intelligent explanation for my apparent about-face concerning Logan,* Marnie silently decided.

The rest of the afternoon passed quickly, as Marnie had back-to-back appointments. She left the office at a little after five and promptly got stuck in rush-hour traffic. Since Marnie lived in the heart of Charleston's historic downtown area, there was no alternate route to be taken.

The more hectic the day, the more Marnie appreciated her antique-filled home. The condominium was actually the converted top floor of what was at one time a wealthy sea captain's house. Rand Sheridan was not only the current-day descendant of that sea captain but also a very talented architect who had turned the dilapidated building into a valuable piece of real estate without violating its architectural heritage. He was also her brother Ben's best friend and a good friend of hers as well.

The Sheridans and Lathropes went way back. Rand's parents and Marnie's were good friends. Despite the miles that often separated the two families as the Lathropes moved from air force base to air force base, they always kept in touch. Now both families were reunited in the Charleston area. Marnie's father had retired from the air force; Rand's from the navy. It seemed natural that when Rand had undertaken the renovation project he should offer one of the condominiums to Ben. But as the proud father of triplets, Ben, with his newly enlarged family, had needed more room. Consequently Rand had offered the place to Marnie.

"I don't want anyone messing up the beautiful work I've done in here," Rand had told her. "I know you won't install track lighting and high-tech junk. Besides, Ben assures me you can sleep through my hammering while I complete the other two units."

Aside from her temper, Marnie's ability to sleep through

anything was another source of family teasing. Ben claimed that she'd slept through an entire typhoon in Taiwan once, one of the many exotic locations she'd grown up in, thanks to her father's varied air force postings. Marnie excused her inattention by pointing out that she'd only been three at the time.

Thinking of her older brother made her wonder what Ben would think of Logan McCallister. And thinking of Logan McCallister made her realize she had only an hour to get ready for their date!

Marnie hurriedly kicked off her navy pumps and padded barefoot into her bedroom. She walked past the four-poster and headed directly for her closet. There she efficiently riffled through her dresses until she found the one she was looking for. The diamond-patterned apricot georgette was a new purchase, one she'd been saving for a special occasion.

Marnie went all out in her preparations. Looking into the mirror forty-five minutes later, she gave a nod of satisfaction. From the top of her newly washed and curled hair to the tip of her stocking-encased toes, she felt as good as she looked. A careful application of makeup had concealed the freckles that were the price she paid for being a redhead. At least her hair was dark enough to go well with apricot, one of her favorite colors, as the color scheme of her living room attested. After adding another coating of lip gloss, she tossed her keys and wallet into a clutch, slipped on a pair of strappy summer sandals, and left to the accompaniment of hammering from downstairs.

The drive to the restaurant was a short one. Marnie arrived at two minutes to seven, congratulating herself on her punctuality.

"A table for one?" the young hostess asked as Marnie walked into the darkened foyer.

"No. I'm waiting for someone else," Marnie told her. "Logan McCallister. Has he arrived yet?"

The hostess showed no sign of recognizing Logan's name. "No, he hasn't checked in with me."

"I'll just wait here, then." Marnie pointed to a vinyl-covered couch.

"Fine." The hostess moved on to the next patrons.

When Logan was fifteen minutes late, Marnie began to feel mild irritation. Perhaps he was delayed in traffic, or perhaps he was having difficulty locating the restaurant. When the fifteen minutes grew to thirty, her excuses dwindled and her irritation grew.

She approached the hostess again. "Excuse me, could you tell me if any messages have been left for me? My name is Marnie Lathrope."

"I'll check." The hostess slipped behind the tall podium that served as her reservations station. "No, I'm sorry, there's no message. Would you be more comfortable waiting at a table?"

"No, thanks." Marnie had no intention of sitting stranded in the dining room. "I'll wait here a while longer."

Marnie watched the people come and go, with something bordering on compulsion. Just as a gambler believes his next quarter will win the jackpot at the slot machine, Marnie was sure that the moment she left, Logan would show up. When he was an hour late, however, she was no longer interested in the jackpot. In fact, she didn't care if, or when, Logan McCallister showed up. She was leaving!

By the time she arrived at work the next morning, Marnie had resolved never to mention Logan's name again. But before Marnie could inform Elaine of this new policy, Elaine was asking her, "How did things go with Logan McCallister?"

Marnie stepped into the elevator they'd been waiting for and roughly punched the button for their floor. "Would telling you that I don't want to hear the man's name even mentioned give you a clue about my feelings on the subject?"

Elaine looked at her friend in confusion. "It went that badly at the banquet?"

"The banquet?" Marnie repeated with a blank frown.

"Isn't that what we're talking about?"

"No."

"Oh. What are we talking about?"

"Never mind." Marnie saw no point in telling Elaine about last night's disaster. Elaine would only have questioned her agreeing to go out with Logan in the first place.

Little did she know that Elaine was wondering why the two people she'd gone to so much trouble to pair up had apparently not stayed paired. The reports Elaine had gotten back from her cousin, Dave Mileson, had seemed to indicate that Logan and Marnie had hit it off despite their differences. So what had gone wrong?

"The banquet went well," Marnie was saying. "The audience seemed to be very responsive to the ideas I brought up."

"The feedback we've gotten here is that things went *very* well. You more than held your own against a professional communicator like McCallister. In fact, Dr. Chapman said that several local high-school principals have requested that you speak at their schools," Elaine told her. "Apparently the superintendent of schools was present at that banquet and you made quite an impression."

As they walked past Diane's desk in the reception area, Marnie was stopped. "Logan McCallister called twice this morning. He said it's important." With one hand Diane handed Marnie the pink message slip with Logan's phone number written on it while with the other hand she answered the ringing phone. "Just a moment, Mr. McCallister. I'll see if she's in." Diane put Logan on hold and looked to Marnie for guidance.

Marnie's first instinct was to say no, but her professional sense of fairness took precedence. There was a slim chance that Logan might have a valid excuse for not showing up last night. Then again, he might be calling about some business matter. He had said it was important. "I'll take the call in my office." She left Elaine shrugging her shoulders at Diane.

Marnie's voice was cool as she spoke into the phone. "This is Dr. Lathrope."

"Marnie, it's Logan." His voice was warmly persuasive, which irritated her.

"Yes, I know. I'm very busy at the moment, Logan. What did you want?"

"You."

Marnie took the phone away from her ear and looked at the receiver as if it had grown horns. This man was incredible! After standing her up and giving no sign of apology, he had the gall to announce bluntly that he wanted her. Returning the mouthpiece to her lips, she strove to keep her temper under control. "Is this the important matter you had to discuss with me?"

"Yes."

"Then allow me to save us both some time and aggravation. I'm not interested, Mr. McCallister. Goodbye."

When Marnie collected the file of her first patient from Diane's desk, she told the receptionist not to put through any more calls from Logan McCallister.

That evening after work Elaine and Marnie left the medical center together and headed for the parking lot and their respective cars. They were discussing one of Elaine's patients, when Elaine abruptly broke off and stared at something over Marnie's right shoulder. The something turned out to be Marnie's car, whose hood displayed an unexpected ornament—a man, a very sexy man!

He was leaning against the front bumper looking for all the world as if he belonged there. He cut a magnetically attractive figure in his light blue western-style shirt and a pair of dark blue denims. The mirror lenses of a pair of sunglasses shielded his eyes from view, giving him a certain casual, even ingenuous glamour. A gentle Charleston breeze tousled the dark strands of his hair.

Elaine spoke first. "Logan McCallister, I presume?"

Logan stood and strolled over with his hand outstretched. "That's right. And you are?"

"Dr. Elaine Casper."

"Another psychologist?" Logan asked.

Elaine nodded. "That's right."

"My guesswork is improving," he murmured with an appealing grin. "Did Marnie tell you about the trouble I had finding her at the banquet the other night?"

Elaine frowned in confusion. "You had trouble finding her?"

"He thought Dave Mileson was the shrink," Marnie explained, using Logan's term.

"I see." Actually Elaine didn't, but she had every intention of pressing Marnie for details later on. For the moment she said, "Well, I'll leave you two alone." On the point of turning away and leaving Marnie to the lone wolf, Elaine casually added one last comment over her shoulder: "However, I feel it only fair to warn you, Mr. McCallister, that Marnie's father is a retired Air Force general with enough clout to get you canned, and her older brother is an expert in the martial arts, so I'm sure you'll treat her with kid gloves. Good night, all."

Marnie watched Elaine's departure in disbelief.

"Nice friend you've got there" was Logan's laughing comment.

"What are you doing here?" Marnie demanded.

"Waiting for you." He removed his sunglasses and proceeded to caress her with his eyes.

"You're wasting your time." She pulled her car keys from her purse, intent on ignoring him.

Logan was equally intent. He grabbed her attention by first grabbing hold of her hand.

"What are you doing?" Her face was flushed with anger.

"Taking you out to dinner." He then proceeded to gently, but purposefully, tug her across the parking lot.

"Our dinner date was last night." Marnie's resentment was evident in her voice as well as her expression.

"I know. I'm sorry about that."

"And I wouldn't exactly call this treating me with kid gloves." Marnie dug in her heels and stopped their forward motion. "I don't appreciate being stood up. If you needed to cancel, you could have phoned me ahead of time instead of making me wait at the restaurant." In her anger Marnie's accent, which she'd acquired in the two years she'd lived in Charleston, had become even more noticeable.

Far from being intimidated by her outburst, Logan seemed entranced by the lyrical flow of her voice. "You know, in these circumstances, I think the name Scarlett might suit you even better than Red."

Marnie looked at him as if he were in need of a straitjacket. "Is that all you've got to say?"

"No. I've got a lot more to say, none of which can be said in a parking lot, however. So, in you get, Scarlett," Logan ordered as he bundled her into his dark green Datsun.

The moment he slammed the door, Marnie's fingers searched out and finally found the door-release handle. The only problem was, it didn't work. The metal mechanism was jammed.

When Logan slid in behind the steering wheel, she expressed her anger through biting sarcasm. "Nice car you've got here."

"Thank you." He accepted the intended insult as if it were a compliment. "I like it."

"Well, I don't, so let me out."

"Can't do that." Logan started the engine.

"You mean you won't."

"That's right." His voice was infuriatingly congenial. "I won't."

"Why?"

"Because I need to talk to you."

"All right," Marnie conceded. "I'll talk to you. On one condition."

"I hate to be blunt, Scarlett, but you're not exactly in a position to be laying down conditions."

"I'm losing my temper," she said warningly.

Logan was not impressed. "Welcome to the club! I lost my temper when you hung up on me this morning. Having you refuse my calls all day did nothing to help me regain it either."

"I told you I'm not interested."

Magically Logan's voice softened. "I know you did, Scarlett. Forgive me for not believing you."

Marnie didn't know what to say to that, so she studied the passing scenery instead. "Where are we going?"

"To a fantastic seafood place I know of." Seeing her mutinous expression, he added, "It's either that or I make love to you here in the car."

She glared at him and deliberately drawled, "Then by all means let's eat."

The corners of Logan's mouth lifted in a smile, the first

he'd displayed since abducting her.

The restaurant Logan had chosen was small and unpretentious. Its proximity to the ocean ensured that the seafood would be freshly caught. A smiling waitress waved them over to a table near a large picture window framing an ever-changing seascape. The early-summer evening held the promise of several more hours of slanting sunlight.

Logan helped Marnie remove her suit jacket and carefully arranged the linen garment over the back of her seat. It was no coincidence that his fingers brushed across the top of her shoulders on more than one occasion. When he took his own seat across from her, Marnie's nerves were quivering. "What would you like?" Logan voiced his seemingly innocent question over the top of the plastic menu.

"To do you bodily harm," Marnie muttered darkly.

To which he tenderly replied, "Not here, darling," just loudly enough for their waitress to overhear.

The waitress shot Marnie an envious look and asked flirtatiously, "Is he taken?"

"Only with himself," Marnie retorted.

Logan insisted on waiting until after they'd eaten their flounder en papillote—a house specialty—before going into what he called the heavy explanations. As they lingered over coffee—it was an aromatic brew—Marnie couldn't help but notice the restless movement of Logan's well-shaped hands as he absently toyed with his spoon.

Catching her eyes on him, he spoke: "I'm sorry I stood you up last night, but something came up."

Marnie had no intention of making it easy for him. "So you said."

Logan took a deep breath and cast his eyes heavenward. "You're really being difficult about this, you know. Will you hear me out?"

"You haven't given me much of a choice. Do you do this sort of thing very often?"

Logan suddenly lost his patience. "If you mean do I ask women out and then forget the name of the restaurant where we'd agreed to meet, then the answer is no. I haven't done that very often. In fact, last night was a first."

It took her a moment to grasp the gist of what he'd said. "You forgot the name of the restaurant?"

"That's what I said."

"Then why didn't you call me and ask me where we were supposed to meet?"

"I did call, but you'd already left. I tried again several times, but you weren't home." He shot her an almost accusatory look.

Marnie felt no need to explain that she'd gone on to a movie last night in an attempt to cheer herself up after he'd stood her up.

"I was on the air at eleven," Logan continued, "doing the lead-in for the report on life insurance scams that I'm covering this week. I figured it was too late to call you after the broadcast."

She'd seen him on the television last night looking vigorously healthy, which had dispelled her fears that he'd been involved in an accident of some sort. But that image had also served to heighten her feelings of resentment, both at him for not showing up and at herself for caring so much!

Yet some parts of his explanation still didn't jibe. The psychologist in her couldn't help wondering if Logan's loss of memory reflected an unconscious desire to bow out of the date. After all, the restaurant's name wasn't a difficult one to remember. She voiced her fears aloud: "Perhaps forgetting where you were supposed to meet me was subconsciously intentional on your part."

"God save me from psychological analysis," he muttered with a growl of exasperation.

Marnie retaliated with a tart rejoinder: "It sounds to me as if you saved yourself, by conveniently forgetting the name of the restaurant and not showing up last night."

"I wasn't myself yesterday." Logan rapped out the words, giving them a clipped inflection.

In contrast, Marnie's southern drawl was even more apparent as she asked softly, "Then who were you?"

"A man who'd gone without a cigarette for twenty-four hours, cold turkey!"

Abruptly the pieces fell into place. "Is that what this is all about?"

In his sensitized state Logan didn't take very well to her initial incredulity. "Forgive me for displaying a natural reluctance to make a fool of myself in front of you, for not wanting you to see me as a nervous wreck. But then, you're used to nervous wrecks, aren't you, Doctor? You deal with them all the time, right? Cold sweats, the shakes." His derisive gaze focused on the hand he held out for her inspection. Sure enough, his lean fingers did display a slight tremor. "Well? Aren't you going to say anything, Doctor?"

Answering a call more powerful than words, her fingers slid between his to offer comfort. "I'm sorry you're in discomfort," she murmured softly.

His face relaxed into a mocking grin. "Are you going to offer me sex as an antidote?"

Now that she had her temper under control, Marnie recognized his baiting techniques. "I'm not into sex as an antidote," she tossed back with an easy smile.

He leaned closer to her to ask, "What are you into?"

"The tartar sauce." His eyes followed hers to the tip of her elbow, which was indeed in the small dish of sauce. Ruefully

41

lifting her billowy sleeve away from its inappropriate resting place, Marnie murmured, "I don't believe I did that."

"Allow me." Logan drew her hand over to his side of the table so that her arm was stretched out between them. With his free hand he pulled a clean paper napkin from the metal holder on their table. Dunking it into his untouched glass of ice water, he dabbed at the stained sleeve of her blouse.

Marnie shivered.

"Too cold?" Logan asked.

Too hot! she silently corrected him. She was suddenly burning up inside, and her internal fires were directly attributable to his touch. *More, more!* She may not have spoken the words aloud, but her sensual gaze spoke for her eloquently. Eyes the color of sherry stared into hers, reading her feelings and returning them.

Singed by the contact, Marnie shakily withdrew her arm. "Thanks."

"No problem." Crushing the damp napkin, Logan abruptly asked, "Are there any men in your life I should know about?"

Marnie blinked at the abrupt change of subject. "What kind of question is that?"

"A direct one. How about making your answer the same." Accompanied as it was by his implacable stare, his statement was in no way a question. No, it was an order of the highest kind.

It was an order Marnie ignored. "Why should you know anything about my life?"

"Let's not play games. You already know the answer to that." His eyes fastened on the pulse point hammering at the base of her collarbone. "You just felt it when I touched you."

Marnie couldn't help it. She raised a hand to shield her telltale fluttering pulse and ended up looking like an

eighteenth-century heroine. "That doesn't give you the right
. . ." Her voice trailed off as she realized that she was also
sounding like one. She then proceeded to confuse Logan to-
tally by breaking into laughter.

"It's not you," she hastily assured Logan amid spurts of
warm laughter. "I'm laughing at myself."

The indignation she'd seen building in his eyes subsided
and was replaced with more than a gleam of humor. "You're
an amazing lady, you know that, Scarlett?"

"Oh, absolutely. It's a requirement in my profession."

Seeing that she had no intention of discussing her private
life, Logan astutely decided to begin by questioning her
about her work. "What made you go into psychology?"

"Trite as this sounds, I wanted to help people."

"It must be very rewarding to see positive results in your
patients."

"Yes, it is. It's also equally disappointing to know there
are some people I simply can't help."

"What made you choose psychology over psychiatry?"

"You want the truth?"

"Absolutely."

"My stomach."

"What?" His eyes slid down her torso to that portion of her
abdomen which he could see. "It looks fine to me." Slim and
firm, just waiting for his hands to caress her. *We'll get to that
later, my dear Scarlett!*

"I meant that I didn't have the stomach for dissecting
frogs," Marnie explained, "let alone operating on people."
She wrinkled her nose in a grimace that Logan found utterly
adorable. "Since psychiatry involved completing medical
school, I opted for clinical psychology instead."

"That's the only difference between a psychologist and a
psychiatrist?" Logan questioned, intent on keeping her

talking. He was becoming addicted to the sound of her voice.

"Not the only difference, no, but the largest one. That's the reason only a psychiatrist is allowed to prescribe drugs."

Determined to find out more about her private life, he casually questioned, "What do you do in your spare time?"

"I don't actually have much spare time," she admitted. "I'm on call at the medical center several evenings a week and one weekend each month. I also do volunteer counseling for the YWCA, which refers battered women to me. Of course, as soon as the shelters open I'll be basing my counseling practice there."

"Shelters?" Logan quickly picked up on that. "I wasn't aware that there would be more than one."

"We'll only have one shelter open at a time, but its location may have to change for obvious reasons."

Logan didn't like the sound of that at all. "Obvious reasons?" His rich voice was ominously quiet.

"For the safety of the shelter's residents."

"What about the safety of the shelter's volunteer counselors?"

"We can take care of ourselves."

"I disagree." Logan jerked the wooden toothpick he'd been restlessly gnawing on and tossed the remnants into an ashtray. *God, but he'd love to have a cigarette about now.* "Let's go."

"Fine." Marnie realized the cause for his moody abruptness and tried to make allowances. Breaking off any habit was an extremely difficult process, and smoking was no exception. In fact, one of her old college classmates had opened a program geared specifically to helping smokers kick the habit. Perhaps she should give Dan a call and see if he had any words of advice that might help Logan.

While she'd been thinking, Logan had taken care of the

bill and was now helping her out of her chair. His hand was warm on the still-damp outline of her elbow as he guided her out of the restaurant. Darkness had fallen while they'd talked inside, and the sound of the waves wafted to them from a seemingly black void. Just then the moon decided to peek out from behind a passing cloud and bathed everything in a celestial glow.

Marnie wouldn't have minded kicking off her sandals and sinking her feet into the sand for a leisurely walk along the wide beach, but Logan seemed intent on bundling her back into his car. Perhaps she'd bored him with her talk about her work. Or worse yet, perhaps she'd scared him off. Marnie had occasionally run across men who were uncomfortable about her profession, appearing to be frightened that she'd in some way analyze them or their performance. Yet Logan didn't seem to be the type of man who would be frightened of anything short of global warfare!

Her eyes drifted over Logan's profile in the dimly lit interior of the sports car as it scooted down the highway. Dark hair casually tumbled over a forehead that was broad and intelligent. The light from a passing car cast shadows across his features, dramatically emphasizing the lean bone structure of his face. His chin may have appeared stubborn, but the shape of his lips was ruled by equal parts of determination and compassion.

While Marnie had been studying Logan, he'd been studying the road in search of an appropriate turnoff. He had found one and was now following the gravel drive to its eventual termination on the beach. Once there, Logan cut the car's engine and flicked off the headlights before delivering the husky pronouncement "I want you, Marnie Lathrope."

CHAPTER THREE

All right, Marnie. Here you are, on a secluded beach, locked in a sports car with a sexy man who's just told you he wants you. What do you say?

"How does that make you feel?" The words were out of her mouth before she'd even realized it. Damn! The psychologist in her had seen a vacuum and had verbally leapt into it. Her front teeth worried her bottom lip as she uneasily awaited Logan's reaction.

It came within three seconds. "I'll show you how it makes me feel!" He dragged her hand over to his chest, positioning her open palm directly over his heart. "Do you feel that?" Logan demanded in a throaty growl.

Marnie answered with a half-strangled "Yes." She could feel his heartbeat and a great deal more! She could feel the warmth of his skin through the cotton of his shirt, feel the rise and fall of his breathing, feel the vivid imprint of his fingers on her hand. She could also feel the effect that touching him had on the rest of her body as ripples of passionate awareness shot through her nervous system.

He spoke her name, turning it into a potent invitation: "Marnie. . . ."

She not only heard the raspy depth of his voice but experienced it through her fingertips, the sound waves traveling up her arm and down her spine. Her dazed eyes finally lifted from the site of their clasped hands, ascending the tanned column of his throat to dwell on the sensual shape of his lips. They were slightly parted as he drew in ragged breaths of air.

Marnie watched spellbound as those lips moved closer to hers, moving in exquisitely slow motion. Soon the air between them was replaced by the living, breathing warmth of their bodies. Now Marnie's lips were parted as her breathing took on the uneven cadence of his. Warm puffs of his breath ricocheted off her moist mouth, signaling his ever-increasing nearness to a mind that had long since given up rational thought.

When Logan was so close that her eyes could no longer focus on him, she shut them. Now a tantalizing darkness enclosed her, cocooning her in its tempting depths. Her heart was racing, her limbs were trembling, and Logan had yet to kiss her!

Uncertain if she could stand the suspense a moment longer, Marnie nervously licked her lips—only to have the intimate gesture erotically repeated by Logan. The coiled tip of his tongue tentatively courted the outer corners of her mouth before seeking permission to woo her throbbing lower lip, to address her trembling upper lip. Provocative gasps of pleasure left her throat and were consumed by him as he finally brushed his mouth across hers. Back and forth, now touching and now retreating, Logan played her senses to their fullest capacity.

Marnie's hands eagerly crept up his chest, scaling his shoulders to reach the base of his neck, where her splayed fingers dug into his hair. Her attempts to transform his tantalizing but fleeting caresses into more satisfying lingering ones were soon rewarded.

His hunger made urgent by the appetizing nibbles he'd had of her, Logan lifted his mouth one more time before shifting and lowering it to utterly consume her. No time was needed, or given, for the usual adjustments that a first kiss requires. Instead they merged lips with the sensual expertise of longtime lovers. Shafts of fire seared their way into Marnie's soul, burning away her inhibitions.

When Logan's tongue evocatively probed her mouth, her tongue responded by making seductive raids of its own, testing the warm taste of his mouth—a mouth she found much to her liking. Their tongues were soon engaged in a passionately undulating encounter that didn't stop until their air-starved lungs cried out for respite. Even then Logan's lips left hers with marked reluctance.

His skin was damp with perspiration as he leaned his forehead against hers, his nose gently nuzzling hers. "My God!" His husky invocation held a kind of marveling wonder. "I have never gotten that much from a kiss before."

Marnie, who was afraid to test her vocal cords, could only nod in silent agreement.

"Can you imagine what it will be like when we make love?" His voice was as dark and sensual as black velvet. "To feel you welcoming me, closing around me. God, lady, you burn me up inside!"

His evocative words hadn't exactly left her unaffected either! Aftershocks of desire were still wreaking havoc with what little self-control she had left. But along with the smoldering passion came the realization that fires burn, and earthquakes devastate. If she let him, Logan McCallister was likely to do both to her.

"I think we need some fresh air." She fumbled with the door handle, forgetting that it was broken.

"Calm down," he said gently. "I'll let you out."

Only when Logan moved away did she realize that they hadn't even been truly embracing each other. The kiss itself had been the focal point of all that towering emotion and prodigious passion. In that context the extent of their reaction was awesome indeed.

Imagine what it would have been like had he held her in his arms, and had she held him in return. Her breasts resting against his chest, her lips molded to his. "Any more imagining and you're going to blow a fuse," Marnie muttered under her breath, fanning her hot cheeks with her hand.

While those thoughts ran through Marnie's head, Logan made his way around the car and opened the passenger door for her from the outside, as he had done at the restaurant. Although Marnie had second thoughts about accepting his offered hand, she took it anyway, telling herself that the low-slung sports car made such assistance necessary.

That rationalization was quickly forgotten as now she found herself under Logan's ministering hand. He helped her from the car and ran his fingers across her flushed cheek.

"Did it get too warm for you, Scarlett?"

His teasing brought her to her senses. Self-protective resolve stiffened a feminine backbone that was in danger of melting. *Snap out of it, Marnie. You've told your patients about the dangers of love at first sight, about the importance of making rational decisions. Yet here you are—doing exactly what you warned them not to do.*

"I don't appreciate being kept captive." Stepping away from Logan, Marnie drew a healthy dose of sea air into her lungs and lifted her face to the refreshing breeze blowing off the ocean.

The romantic surroundings didn't provide her with much inspiration for cool restraint, however. The sound of the thundering surf was too reminiscent of the thundering of Logan's heart. The lazy moon that dallied on the water's edge also lit Logan's face. And the salty heaviness of the sea air teased her nostrils with the haunting memory of Logan's scent.

"Captive?" Logan was questioning. "After that kiss I'm not sure who's keeping whom captive."

She could not imagine Logan ever being unsure about anything.

"Come on, let's go for a walk." He grabbed hold of her hand and then released it.

Marnie felt an astonishing degree of loss in that moment.

"Wait here a second. I want to get something else out of the car." He opened the door and pulled a folded blanket out of the backseat. "There. Let's go." He walked over and took her hand again.

"These shoes weren't designed for walking on the beach," she protested.

"Then take them off."

She reluctantly did so and let the sandals dangle from her free hand. Her cautionary "I do have to be getting back soon" was meant as much for her benefit as his.

"Scared?" he taunted.

"Petrified," she replied, half kidding, half serious.

She knew her natural response had pleased Logan immensely, but it had also given him entirely the wrong impression. Marnie knew herself well enough to know she couldn't handle going to bed with a man on one day's acquaintance, no matter how fantastic a kisser he might be!

Besides, reality was filtering through the diminishing clouds of passion. What did she have in common with Logan, a man who moved from issue to issue, from city to city, in search of a better story, a bigger audience?

Mind over matter, that's all it takes, Marnie. Explain yourself to him and maybe you can still part friends.

"Logan . . ."

"I want to do a story about your shelter, Marnie."

Those words were the last she'd expected to hear from him at that moment. "Why are you telling me this now?"

"Because I don't want you misinterpreting my actions."

His actions? Like kissing her in his car, for example? "Then why don't you explain your actions to me, that way there won't be any chance of misinterpretation." She was pleasantly astonished to hear the steady calmness in her voice, especially in light of the painful thumping of her heart.

"All right." Logan stopped walking and turned to face her. "I don't want you jumping to the incorrect conclusion that my interest in you revolves around this story. In fact, the opposite may be true."

She would not try to guess his motivations. It would be simpler, Marnie decided, to ask bluntly, "Why do you want to do a story on the shelter?"

"The story I did on family violence turned up some surprising statistics, some of which you've already quoted to me. The idea of doing a more in-depth study has been knocking around in the back of my mind ever since. Besides, this may be my chance to prove to you that television journalism can be a noble profession." He ended on a note of levity. "So what do you say?"

As she did whenever the topic of battered women or the shelter was raised, Marnie adopted a serious tone. "What exactly would doing this story entail?"

"Once the shelter opens I'd like to interview you there along with some of the residents—"

"No," she interrupted emphatically. "Any interviews with me would have to be done in my office at the medical center, and then only after I'd gotten permission from Dr. Chapman. As for the future residents—"

"I realize I'd have to wait until the shelter opens," Logan inserted, incorrectly anticipating her protest.

"You'll have to wait forever." In the moonlight her face took on an unexpectedly determined expression. "The residents, when we get them, will not need a microphone jammed in their face and a reporter asking them 'How does it feel to be beaten, Mrs. Smith?' "

"Grant me more sensitivity than that," Logan retorted, angered by her prejudgment of him.

Marnie sighed. She hadn't meant to come on so strong. "You know what I mean."

"I'm afraid I do," he answered with a dose of bitterness. "For a psychologist, you sure have a lot of misconceptions about reporters."

"I've seen it happen before, Logan."

Something in her voice softened his response. "When?"

"It's a long story."

"I've got time. And I've got this." Unfolding the plaid blanket, Logan shook it out and spread it on the sand. He settled down, patting the space beside him. "Come on down here." He waited until she was sitting beside him before saying, "Tell me about it."

"Off-the-record?"

"Yes, off-the-record." His sigh held equal amounts of impatience and exasperation. Holding his arms out wide, he asked, "Sure you don't want to frisk me for a tape recorder?"

Marnie shook her head.

"Too bad," he murmured ruefully. "So tell me."

"I got my PhD at the University of Michigan in Ann Arbor." She could sense his surprise.

"You went to a northern university, Scarlett?"

"I haven't lived in Charleston all my life," she retorted wryly. Far from it, as a matter of fact. But that was not pertinent to the story she was telling him now. "My alma mater boasts one of the best psychology programs in the country. As part of my internship program I worked in a shelter for abused women in Detroit. The local news decided to do a special on wife beating, and the people running the shelter agreed to let them film the residents, providing they consented, of course."

"Did the residents consent?"

Marnie nodded slowly. "A few did."

"What happened?"

"Some hotshot reporter—it happened to be a woman because the station thought she'd have more insight into the situation—jammed a microphone into a resident's still-bruised face and asked her how it felt to be beaten. Was it true that battered wives enjoyed it? Is that why she'd stayed with her husband for so long?"

Logan swore under his breath. Much as he hated to admit it, there were times when some of his colleagues could be real asses.

"I'll never forget the look on that poor woman's face." Marnie shuddered even now. "The tape was never aired, but the damage was done. That attitude—the mistaken idea that women enjoy being beaten—is surprisingly pervasive."

His fingers reached out to ease open the hand that she had automatically clenched into a fist. "Marnie, helping me do a segment would be your chance to reach thousands of people and correct those misconceptions they have about battered women."

"You'd really have to speak to the organizers at the Women's Coalition, Logan. I'm only a small cog in the wheel that's gotten the shelter moving. Those women are really the driving force behind the project."

"How do I get in touch with them?"

Marnie thought a moment before saying, "Give me your card and I'll have them get in touch with you."

"Cautious to the end, aren't you?" Despite his good-natured grumbling, Logan dipped his fingers into his back pocket, brought out his wallet, and flipped it open. Extracting two cards, he then balanced them on his now closed wallet in order to write a brief note with the pen he'd pulled from his shirt pocket. Then he handed the cards to Marnie, one at a time. "This one is for the Women's Coalition." He handed her another card, this time making sure his fingers lingered over hers. "And this one is for you." He watched her squint in the faint light as she tried to make out what he'd written. "I wrote my home phone number on yours. It's unlisted, so don't lose it."

"I don't make a habit of losing things." She felt compelled to defend herself.

"Good. Neither do I." His gaze, even in the softened moonlight, clearly told her that he considered *her* one of the things he had no intention of losing.

Marnie, on the other hand, had no intention of becoming immersed in another passionate encounter. "It's getting late." She rose gracefully to her feet. "I've got to get back."

Logan surprised her by making no protest and readily driving her back to the parking lot of the medical center, where she'd left her car. He also surprised her with his silence during the twenty-minute trip. The car's custom stereo filled the void with the sound of Dan Fogelberg.

When Logan stopped his car beside hers, he switched off the stereo but not the engine. "Before you leave, there's just one more thing, Marnie."

"What's that?"

"I wasn't kidding when I said I want you. And now that I know you want me too—"

"I never said that," Marnie denied heatedly, angry because she'd allowed herself to be lulled into thinking he'd forgotten about the explosive kiss they'd shared.

"You didn't have to." His soft inflection fell soothingly on her ears. "The way you kissed me said it all."

"I wanted to explain about that. . . ."

"Actions speak louder than words," Logan murmured. His hand reached out to caress the bared curve of her knee. "And, Scarlett, your actions were enough to melt steel!"

Marnie returned his hand to the steering wheel and elegantly flicked the hem of her front-buttoning skirt into a more decorous arrangement. "It wasn't my intention to melt steel," she informed him aloofly.

"No? Then what are your intentions?"

"To get out of this car without any further . . . entanglements."

In the artificial illumination provided by the parking-lot lights, Marnie could see Logan's thoughtful nod. "Mmm, yes, I suppose that would be for the best. As it is, I'll have to take a cold shower when I get home, and even then, I'll probably dream about making love to you all night."

As a psychologist Marnie was accustomed to having people tell her all sorts of intimate details about their lives. Why was it, then, that she blushed like a schoolgirl whenever Logan teased her with flirtatious statements? Marnie came no closer to finding an answer to her question while driving home. Caught up as she was in her thoughts, she didn't notice the pair of headlights tailing her.

She parked her white Chrysler in the narrow drive that had once carried horse-drawn carriages over its uneven surface. The front of the house was dark as she walked past it to her own private entrance near the back. Suddenly the porch light was switched on and the front door thrown open.

Rand, dressed in jeans and a green T-shirt, came clambering down the front steps and caught her up in a bear hug. "They came, they finally came!"

"Rand!" Marnie gasped in surprise. "Put me down! My shoes are falling off!"

Rand had swung her around once more before her words sank in. Then he carefully set her back on her own two feet.

From the street the scene looked ominously romantic to the man sitting in the dark green 280Z. "So much for chivalrous instincts, McCallister," Logan muttered derisively. Wanting to make sure Marnie made it home all right, he'd followed her, never expecting her to lead him to the heart of Charleston's historic district—and to a huge mansion complete with a man.

The spiky shadow of a palm tree flickered over Logan's face as he abruptly reached into the glove compartment in search of a cigarette. *Damn!* He came up with a dollar bill, a stack of McDonald's paper napkins, and a very feminine article of clothing. But no cigarettes.

The Datsun's engine made the transition from park to drive with a smooth purr that the two people standing in the pool of light from the house didn't even notice.

Having regained her breath, Marnie said, "All right, Rand. What's up?"

"Those authentic bathroom fixtures I was waiting for finally showed up!"

"Great." Marnie surreptitiously slid her left foot back into her shoe.

"Great?" Rand repeated. "It's fantastic! I've been waiting for those fixtures for six months. Now I can finally get to work on the downstairs bathroom."

"I suppose that means you're going to be messing with the water again, huh? Turning it off at the most inconvenient moments." The last time Rand had worked on the plumbing, he'd turned the water off while Marnie was in the shower washing her hair. She hadn't appreciated being stranded with a headful of soapsuds.

"This time I'll give you advance warning before I do anything," Rand assured her. "Hey, isn't that your phone?"

Marnie had left her windows open to catch the cooling breeze from the harbor and the unusual ringing sound of her phone drifted down to them. "Sure is. Talk to you later, Rand." She hurried upstairs with her key all ready to insert into the lock. She reached her answering machine just as it was completing her recorded message: "Leave your name and number and your call will be returned."

"This is Logan," a low voice growled.

Logan! Marnie punched the answering machine's off button and lifted the receiver. "Hello?"

Unaware that he was now dealing with Marnie live and not via a recording, Logan did not return the greeting. "My message concerns the other men in your life."

"Logan? What are you talking about?"

There was a brief pause before Logan shot back "Who was that man?"

"What man?" she asked patiently.

"The one you were hugging on your front steps," he replied impatiently.

Marnie's mouth dropped open in surprise. "How did you know?"

"Never mind how I knew, just answer my question. Who is he?"

"Rand Sheridan."

"That doesn't tell me a hell of a lot, Marnie." Logan's voice had lowered into an absolute growl. "I want to know what he is to you."

"He's an old friend."

Her answer in no way placated Logan. "He didn't look that old to me."

"Where are you?" Marnie's eyes flickered to the window, as if expecting to find him perched on her windowsill.

"I'm at a pay phone in front of a liquor store."

That sounded ominous. "Have you been drinking?" Marnie tried to delete any sign of suspicion from her question.

"Not yet. I came here to get cigarettes. And don't you dare ask me how that makes me feel," he warned her.

"I wasn't about to."

"Do you realize that you've gotten under my skin so badly that you're even worse than a nicotine attack? I got to the cash register and I couldn't pay for the cigarettes."

Marnie was getting confused. "You ran out of money?"

"No, I ran out of patience. I kept seeing your face, and I knew I wanted you more than I wanted the damn cigarettes. So you'd better tell me what you were doing in another man's arms at eleven at night."

"Rand's antique bathroom fixtures finally arrived."

"What?" His voice was eloquent with disbelief.

"Rand owns this house," Marnie explained, kicking off her shoes and settling down onto the apricot couch. "He's an architect, and he's converting each of the three floors into three condominiums. He was simply excited because he'd been waiting for those fixtures for six months and they'd finally arrived."

"What kind of guy gets excited about bathroom fixtures when you're living in his house?" Logan made no attempt to delete the suspicion from his voice.

"I'm not living in Rand's house," Marnie corrected him. "I'm renting the third-floor condominium while he's completing the other two. Rand's quarters are on the first floor. Besides, he's practically living with a luscious model, although why I'm telling you, I can't imagine."

"I can." Now his voice reflected male satisfaction.

Marnie felt it was time to make a few things clear. "Logan, we've just met. You don't have any claims on me."

"Sure I do. The claim of a man who intends to make love to you."

His answer fairly took her breath away. The last time Marnie had felt this way was when Ben had accidentally kicked a football in her direction and it had landed in the middle of her stomach, knocking all the air from her.

"I just have one more question, Scarlett," Logan whispered seductively into the silence. "Is your father really a retired Air Force general with enough clout to get me canned, and your brother an expert in the martial arts?"

"Sorry, that's two questions," Marnie cooed in return, having regained her breath and sanity. "Good night, Logan."

His husky laughter haunted her dreams that night.

As promised, Marnie called the Women's Coalition from her office first thing the next morning and spoke to Gwen Davis, the group's organizer. "Gwen, this is Marnie Lathrope."

"Yes, Marnie. What can I do for you?"

"Have you heard of Logan McCallister?"

"McCallister? Doesn't he do those focus reports on the eleven-o'clock news?"

"That's right. He wants to do a story on battered women and the shelter."

"I see."

"I said I would pass along that information as well as his number. Do you have a pen and paper?"

"Hold on a second. . . . Yeah, go ahead."

Marnie gave Gwen the number, adding, "I told him you'd get in touch with him if you were interested."

"We're definitely interested," Gwen replied. "The publicity should help our fund-raising efforts. He does understand that he wouldn't be allowed into the shelter itself, doesn't he?"

"I told him that, yes." Knowing Logan, however, she

doubted that he would accept her word as final. "How are things going?"

"We've got the okay to open in three weeks."

"Three weeks!" Marnie's voice reflected her surprise. "But you don't have any furniture for the residents yet, do you?"

"We've gotten a few donations. In fact, one of the other women has a line on some mattresses, so if you've got any extra bed linens, we could use them."

"I'm sure I can come up with something."

"Thanks, Marnie. Don't forget our meeting this weekend." The group met every Saturday to prepare for the shelter's opening.

"I won't," Marnie promised. "See you then."

Elaine popped her head in at the open doorway to the office just as Marnie was hanging up. "You free for lunch today?"

Marnie quickly checked her appointment book before saying "Yes."

"Good. Let's pig out at Andre's."

Marnie smiled at Elaine's choice of words. "What's the occasion?"

"You're going to tell me all about your evening with Logan McCallister and I'm going to make a small confession of my own."

Marnie was intrigued. "Really, tell me more."

"Unh, unh." Elaine shook her head. "You've got to wait until lunchtime, the same as me."

Andre's offered French cuisine in the form of gourmet sandwiches and rich desserts. After a waiter had taken their order, Marnie sipped at her glass of Chablis and said, "You first. What's this confession you were talking about?"

Elaine squeezed a wedge of lime into her glass of Perrier water before answering with a question of her own: "How did things go after I left you last night? Did Logan treat you with kid gloves?"

"I don't know that I'd go quite that far."

"Oh?" Elaine raised an eyebrow. "How far did you go?"

"Far enough!" Marnie took another sip of her wine before muttering "That man is as dangerous as nitroglycerin!"

"Maybe, but nitroglycerin can be very effective for the heart," Elaine pointed out.

"Not in these massive doses." Marnie sat back in her chair with a sigh. "You know, this really isn't like me."

"What isn't?"

"This feeling of overwhelming physical attraction."

"Having seen the guy, it seems to me your reaction is positively normal."

"Normal for a lovesick adolescent maybe, not for a psychologist."

"Wait a minute! It's wrong for psychologists to feel physically attracted to handsome men?"

"It's wrong for this psychologist because Logan and I really don't have anything in common. He doesn't take anything seriously. I don't want to get involved with someone like that."

"I'm really sorry to hear that," Elaine murmured.

"Why's that?"

"Because I went to a great deal of trouble to get you and Logan together."

Surely Elaine couldn't be implying . . . "What are you saying?"

"That my matchmaking attempts seem to have bombed out!" Elaine confessed with wry bluntness.

CHAPTER FOUR

"Matchmaking!" Marnie stared at her friend in disbelief. "You must be kidding!"

"Not at all," Elaine said.

"Who ordered the beef sandwich?" their waiter interrupted them to ask.

"I did," Elaine answered.

"I can't believe this." Marnie shook her head after the waiter departed.

"Believe what? The size of your sandwich—" Elaine's hazel eyes dropped to the delicious-looking creation sitting in front of Marnie—paper-thin slices of ham and melon heaped on a fresh-baked *croissant*. "—or my confession?"

For the moment Marnie ignored the mouth-watering food and concentrated on Elaine. "Your confession. What ever possessed you?"

"It seemed a good idea at the time." Elaine picked up her knife and cut her sandwich into manageable pieces.

"Why?"

"Because Logan McCallister was able to incite passionate feelings in you."

"Feelings of resentment and anger at his biased reporting," Marnie retorted. "I thought you agreed with me."

"I do. I do. I'm not saying that matchmaking was my *only* reason for arranging your appearance at that banquet dinner. I knew you'd be an articulate speaker, the perfect representative to voice our concerns about violence on television news. But I was also hoping you and Logan

62

might be able to resolve your differences."

"As far as the shelter itself is concerned, we have come closer to resolving our differences," Marnie admitted. She enjoyed a healthy bite of her sandwich before adding, "Logan wants to do a series about battered women."

"That's great!"

"Is it? He wanted to interview me at the shelter."

Elaine paused in the act of dipping a corner of her beef sandwich into a cup of gravy. "Did you tell him that wouldn't be possible?"

"Sure I told him. I don't know how seriously he took my words, though."

"You explained the security problems to him?"

"Yes, and he proceeded to lecture me about *my* safety."

"Sounds like the man's interested in you."

"He's interested in women, period," Marnie retorted.

"Mmm," Elaine murmured affirmatively while swallowing the last bite of her sandwich. "I imagine he must have quite a reputation as a ladies' man."

"I don't care what kind of reputation he has. I'm not about to become ruled by spontaneous emotions."

"You're going to rule them, not the other way around, right?"

"Yes. Now if we could vary the subject slightly. . . ."

"Sure."

"Do you think Tom"—Marnie used Dr. Chapman's Christian name—"will approve the idea of my being interviewed at the office?"

"I can't imagine why not, but you won't know for sure until you ask him."

Marnie spoke to Dr. Chapman that very afternoon. The psychiatrist was in his early fifties and had the look of empathy that marked the best counselors. He sat behind his desk and viewed Marnie over the top of his dark-framed reading glasses.

Knowing he was busy, Marnie got right to the point. "As you know, Tom, I'm involved with the shelter for battered women that's going to be opening soon."

"I remember." Tom nodded. "You said you were going to be doing volunteer counseling with the women there."

"That's right."

"Are you having problems with that?"

"Not at all. This concerns another aspect of the shelter. Logan McCallister has informed me of his interest in doing a series of special reports on battered women. And as part of that series, he'd like to interview me. I wanted your thoughts about my doing the interview here at the office. Do you have any objections?"

Tom thought about it for a moment before saying "I don't see any problem with that, as long as the filming is restricted to your office. I don't want any of our patients to be unduly intimidated by the presence of a television crew in our midst."

"Perhaps I could arrange to have the interview done when the office would normally he closed," Marnie suggested.

"That's a possibility, certainly."

It wasn't a possibility, however, as far as Logan was concerned.

"Marnie, getting a crew on a Sunday or for an evening would mean overtime," Logan told her over the phone when she called him at the station. "And the station won't approve that."

"Upsetting our patients is something Dr. Chapman won't approve," Marnie retorted.

"Your patients won't even know we're there," Logan promised. "We'll set up in your office, so no one in the waiting room will be exposed to the camera at all. Will this be your first televised interview?" He slid the question in.

"Yes."

"In that case, perhaps we should meet to discuss the line of questioning."

Taken at face value, Logan's request sounded logical enough. But to clarify the matter, she said, "I'll agree, on one condition."

"What's that?"

"That we keep the discussion on a professional level." Her tone was polite but firm.

"And keep *ourselves* away from a horizontal level, is that it?" he drawled with intentional bluntness.

Why did she bother using courtesy with this man? "Crassly put, yes."

"What are you afraid of, Scarlett?" His voice dropped to a silky growl. "That maybe I'll melt that chilly facade of yours?"

"Put it down to a natural aversion to being burned," Marnie wryly declared.

Logan pounced on that: "Then you admit I do get to you?"

"The sun gets to me, too, and has an equally bad effect on me," she retorted with tart humor. "So do you agree to my condition?"

"That we keep the discussion on a professional level? Sure, I agree. It won't make any difference in the long run, you know. I'll catch you in the end."

"Logan. . . ." She'd meant it to be a warning, but instead it sounded disconcertingly like a plea.

"We'll talk over dinner."

Marnie hesitated.

"Unless you'd rather I come to your office and we discuss

this there?" he questioned.

Marnie's appointment schedule was already fairly full, she'd have a hard time fitting another appointment in. Besides, she wasn't sure she wanted Logan interrupting her workday. Talking to him on the phone was bad enough!

"Dinner will be fine," she agreed, albeit reluctantly.

"Great. Your place or mine?"

"Neither."

"Don't tell me you're going to suggest that we meet at a restaurant again?"

"Not exactly, no. I thought I'd pick you up at the station."

"*You'd* pick *me* up?" Logan was incredulous.

"Something wrong with that?" Her question was a challenge.

"Nothing at all," Logan denied. "I just never thought you were the type of woman to come after a man."

"While I, on the other hand, expected you to be exactly the type of man who'd make a comment like that," she retorted sweetly.

Logan retaliated with a huskily murmured "If you'd let me, I'm sure I'd be able to live up to *all* your expectations, Scarlett."

"Good or bad?"

"You'd have to be the judge of that," he replied with irrepressible devilment. Then waiting a beat, he modestly added, "I haven't received any complaints so far."

"There's a first time for everything."

He accepted her warning as a sensual promise. "I'm looking forward to our first time. When will you come and get me?"

Marnie resisted the temptation to say "July 1999," and instead suggested "Five forty-five?"

"Fine."

"Where's the station located?"

Logan gave her directions. "I'll be waiting for you, Scarlett."

And he was too. Right outside the building, casually sitting astride a fire hydrant. The late-afternoon sun shone down on him, drawing forth shades of mahogany in his dark hair and enhancing the teak of his tanned skin. His mirror-lensed sunglasses were again in place, shielding his identity from the view of the passing pedestrians. Dressed in khaki pants and a dark blue cotton-knit polo shirt, he looked cool and crisp despite the humid heat of this Charleston summer day.

Marnie suddenly felt sweaty and rumpled in comparison. A swift glance into her rearview mirror served the dual purpose of quelling her fears about her appearance and confirming the safety of moving into the right lane. Her short-sleeved beige mesh top showed no sign of wear, and the traffic was clear behind her. With those two thoughts in mind, Marnie eased her car over to the curb. When Logan showed no sign of getting up, her slender finger activated the automatic control for the window on the passenger side as she prepared to call over to him.

"What is this?" Logan grinned at her from his perch atop the fire hydrant. "A pickup?"

"Are you coming or not?" she demanded, worried about the possibility of getting a ticket for stopping in a no-parking zone.

"I had no idea you were so hot for my body, Scarlett," he murmured mischievously after opening the passenger door and sliding into the seat beside her.

"I'm not hot, Logan. My car's got air-conditioning." She turned the fan on full blast to illustrate her point, even remembering to close the passenger window at the same time.

"Where are you taking me?"

Marnie was pleased by his question. "Now you know how I felt when you abducted me."

"This is how you felt?"

She nodded, and wished she hadn't when he added, "Burning up with sexual needs and desires?"

"No! Of course not."

"Why of course not? Women have sexual needs too. Don't you?"

"I don't think this conversation falls under the category of a professional discussion," she retorted with exasperation.

"I thought it fit right into your profession. Don't psychologists deal with sexual problems?"

"Some do," she replied in a calm voice, refusing to let him throw her. "That isn't my specialty. And to belatedly answer your first question, I thought we'd go to the Rib Joynt."

"The place with the best prime ribs in Charleston?"

"That's the one," she confirmed.

"You must be a mind reader. The idea of prime ribs is high on my list—preceded only by the prospect of nibbling on your ribs."

Marnie found herself smiling as she murmured a mocking riposte: "I'm honored to be placed next to a side of beef in your estimation."

But it was Logan who got in the last word: "I'd rather you were placed next to *my* side."

By this time they'd reached the restaurant, which was heavily frequented by those who appreciated good food.

After they'd been shown to a booth in a darkened corner and had placed their order, Logan asked, "Is it all right with you if we begin the questioning now, while we're waiting for our meal?"

"That's fine."

"Okay." Logan reached into his shirt pocket and extracted a small black notebook. "You got your doctorate degree in psychology from the University of Michigan at Ann Arbor, is that correct?"

Marnie sighed inwardly. Good, Logan was sticking to the ground rules. She could handle him well as long as he stayed on noncontroversial subjects. "Yes."

"And what brought you to Charleston?"

Her relief at his agreeableness made her expansive. "My father retired while I was still in graduate school. He and my mother bought a condo on Kiawah Island. I flew down a couple of times to visit them, and I fell in love with this part of South Carolina. Once I got my degree, I was offered a position with Dr. Chapman's group practice and I accepted."

"How long ago was that?"

"Two years."

He made a brief note in his notebook. From her position across the table Marnie could discern that he was writing in some form of shorthand. "Your father was in the air force?"

"That's right." She took a sip of her ice water so her attention wouldn't remain fixed on Logan's lean fingers.

"How many brothers and sisters do you have?"

Drinking the water didn't help. Her eyes slid right back to Logan's hand. Hoping to disguise her undue interest, Marnie fixed a bright, interested smile on her face and answered his question. "One older brother, Ben."

"The expert in the martial arts?" Logan looked at her smile and wondered at its cause. Was she imagining him being beaten to a pulp by her brother?

"Ben's got a black belt in karate, but that isn't how he makes his living, no."

That's reassuring, McCallister. No need to get out your karate handbook yet. "What does he do for a living?"

"He develops computer software."

"Here in Charleston?"

"Yes."

"So the whole family's together?"

"Yes."

"Would you say that you're all close?"

"Relatively close, yes."

"How does your family feel about your volunteer work with battered women?"

You walked right into that one, Marnie. Obviously Logan's tactic was to ask the simple questions first, lulling his subject into a false sense of security, and then to pounce. "My family is supportive of all aspects of my career."

"I find it difficult to believe that a retired military man would approve of his daughter involving herself in a potentially dangerous situation." Logan's statement took the form of a taunt.

"Driving a car can be a potentially dangerous situation," Marnie pointed out reasonably. "My father trusts my judgment."

"Ah, but does he approve?"

What was he getting at? "Why this interest in my father?"

"I'm just trying to get an overall picture of your personality," Logan explained with a suspiciously innocent expression. "A character sketch of sorts. Unless my questions about your background bother you?"

"Not at all."

"Good."

"How about you?" Marnie inquired.

"What about me?"

Now it was her turn to play interrogator. "Do questions about your background bother you?"

"Yes," Logan answered bluntly.

70

"Why?" she asked equally bluntly.

"Get that shrink's gleam out of your gorgeous brown eyes, Scarlett," he ordered softly. "I have no intention of baring my soul to you. My body, yes. My soul, no."

"Afraid?" she asked, returning his challenge of the night before.

And he borrowed her reply of that night: "Petrified."

Marnie didn't give up. "Of what?"

"Beautiful lady shrinks with the curves and fiery hair of a Botticelli angel."

"Why do they scare you?" She refused to let him off the hook. "What are you afraid these lady shrinks will do to you?"

"I'm not afraid of what they might do to me," he drawled. "It's what they might *not* do that worries me."

"Might not do?" Marnie repeated in confusion.

"That's right." Logan's voice dropped to a seductive whisper, and his eyes held her in their smoldering depths. "They might not admit to their true feelings, might not confess to the same needs I have, might not accept the powerful magic between us."

So much for trying to put him on the spot, Marnie. The time had obviously come for some plain speaking. "Look, Logan, I think we should be honest here."

"By all means," he agreed.

"The truth is that although I may be physically attracted to you, I've no intention of getting involved with you."

"I know that you don't intend to get involved with me, as you so quaintly put it. But I also know that we will end up together, whatever your intentions."

"How do you figure that?"

His grin was wicked. "Fate. There's just no fighting it."

There was also no fighting Logan's intention of taping the interview as soon as possible. The topic arose after they'd both polished off their generous helpings of prime ribs. Marnie, who'd foreseen the need to set up a mutually agreeable time, had brought along her appointment book. As they lingered over coffee, Marnie was shaking her head over his latest proposal: the day after tomorrow—Friday.

"I've already got patients scheduled all day Friday."

Logan was clearly disgruntled. "What about Monday, then?"

"Monday's not good either. How about Tuesday?"

Logan consulted his own schedule. "No good. Wednesday?"

She nodded. "Wednesday is possible. How about four o'clock?"

"Four is good."

She noted the details in her appointment book, then asked, "You're sure your crew won't be disruptive?"

"No problem—unless, of course, there's a full moon." Logan's expression became darkly somber and his eyes narrowed as he said in his best Transylvanian accent, "Then there's no telling what might happen!"

"In that case, let's pray there's no full moon," she retorted.

That wasn't all Marnie found herself praying for as she drove Logan back to the television studio, where he'd left his car. Her heavenward pleas revolved around the man sitting beside her and the need for her to maintain her distance from him. Exchanging teasing banter was one thing, but as Logan's kiss the night before had already told her, anything beyond that was liable to consume her entirely.

Which was why Marnie took the precaution of leaving the engine running as she pulled over to the curb in front of the building housing the TV station. "Thank you for the dinner, Logan." Despite her protests, he'd insisted on paying for her meal, unequivocally stating that the station would reimburse him for the expense, since it had been a business dinner.

"You're welcome." So abruptly that she had no time to prepare herself, Logan leaned over to plant a firm, startling kiss on her lips. "See ya on Wednesday, Scarlett," he said as he slid out of the car.

As an impatient driver behind her started beeping his horn, Marnie voiced a rueful accusation at the Deity to whom she'd appealed. "You weren't listening!"

As if to repay her for her impish complaint, the heavens opened wide the following Wednesday morning, heralding what promised to be one of the wettest days in Charleston's meteorological history.

Thank goodness Elaine, who had previous experience with television interviews, had spent the evening before counseling Marnie on what to wear.

"Anything but blue."

"How about this?" Marnie held up a paisley dress that was a favorite of hers.

"Too busy. The simpler the better. Black and white looks great in color. So does gray."

"I've got a gray suit with tiny pin stripes." Marnie tugged it from her closet and added it to the pile of clothes already on her bed. "Will this do?"

"Fine. Now, do you have a cream-colored or a pink blouse?"

Marnie returned to the closet and retrieved a short-sleeved vanilla-colored blouse. The polyester georgette material was trimmed with touches of lace.

"Perfect!" Elaine decreed.

"Okay, now that that's settled, what am I going to do about my hair?" Marnie positioned herself in front of the huge oval mirror attached to her mahogany dressing table.

"What's wrong with your hair?"

"It's too . . ." Marnie paused as if searching for a suitable description. All she came up with was "red."

"Your hair is a gorgeous auburn color, not red. Red is the color of a fire engine. Your hair's more like one of those newly minted pennies."

Marnie absently murmured, "That's what Logan said once."

"Really? There may be hope for the man after all!"

Meanwhile Marnie was piling her hair on top of her head, twisting it this way and that in search of the proper look for a psychologist. She didn't want to appear too trendy, or too romantic. Classic elegance was the look she was striving for.

"Maybe I should get a perm," she mused aloud. "Except with my luck I'd come out of the hairdresser's looking like Little Orphan Annie."

"Your hair's just about long enough to pin up into a French plait," Elaine suggested. "That would be cool and sophisticated."

Cool and sophisticated, right. But now monsoon rains threatened to add *wet* and *waterlogged* to that list of adjectives! By the time she got to the medical center Marnie was wishing she'd arranged for the interview to take place at the beginning of the workday, rather than at the end of it.

Diane obviously shared those feelings. "I don't know how I'm going to wait until four o'clock when the TV crew arrives." She handed Marnie her messages. "I'm really looking forward to meeting Logan McCallister. You won't forget to introduce me, will you?"

"I won't forget, Diane."

Elaine stopped by Marnie's office in between patients. "Your suit looks great. I've got to go over to the hospital this afternoon, so I'm going to miss seeing Logan."

"Is it the little boy who had appendicitis?"

Elaine nodded. "There were complications, and now he's afraid he'll never get out of the hospital. He's reverting back to his disruptive behavior patterns."

"If anyone can help, you can, Elaine."

"Thanks for the encouragement, Marnie, and good luck this afternoon." Elaine flashed Marnie a thumbs-up sign before leaving.

In the waiting room Marnie was saying good-bye to her last patient of the day when the elevator doors parted and two passengers got out. The shock of seeing Logan on her home turf, so to speak, was compounded by the fact that it had been a week since she'd seen him at all. Hoping that her attraction to him would diminish if she stayed away from him, she'd even avoided watching his news reports.

But avoidance hadn't helped any, if the force of her heartbeat was anything to go by. To her eyes Logan looked even better than she'd remembered. And in her heart the void that had gnawed at her all week was suddenly filled.

Marnie unconvincingly attributed her symptoms to nervousness as she greeted Logan and his associate. "You're right on time. If you'll both come back to my office . . ."

Marnie remembered her promise to Diane and introduced her to the two men before continuing on to her own office. Once there, the cameraman, whom Logan introduced simply as Joe, immediately began setting up, flipping on a pair of portable quartz lights. In an instant the room was flooded with glaringly brilliant light, and what was, only moments before, a comfortable, inviting environment had taken on the clinically sterile look of an operating room. No wonder Logan wore sunglasses so often, she decided ruefully, forced as he was to work behind those lights. They had probably half blinded him, as they were now blinding Marnie.

75

"Your eyes will adjust in a minute," Joe absently informed her, already engrossed in another piece of equipment.

Adjust? Would she ever adjust to Logan? Not when he looked so incredibly good in cream gabardine pants and an ivory cotton shirt.

"I'm ready here, Logan," Joe announced. "Where do you want her?"

For a brief moment Logan's eyes flashed their erotic answer to Marnie in such explicit detail that she felt the threat of a blush.

"Marnie, why don't you sit behind your desk, and we'll try it from there."

Joe saw nothing unusual in Logan's request, but Marnie did not fail to take note of the *double entendre* with its subliminal message.

The militant set of her jaw warned Logan that she was aware of his underhanded tactics and did not approve of them.

Once she was seated behind her desk, Joe asked her to face left and then right. "That print behind her will have to go," he said. "I'm getting a glare off the glass. And that ceramic pencil holder on her desk clashes with her dress. Move it off there."

Logan took care of the van Gogh print while Marnie moved her pencil holder into the safekeeping of her bottom desk drawer.

Joe again peered into his video camera before pronouncing judgment: "Mmm, better, but your nose is shining, Dr. Lathrope. Do you have some powder?"

Great, just great. If this was the world of broadcasting, they could keep it. As if Marnie hadn't been nervous enough before, now she felt as conspicuous as Rudolph the Red-nosed Reindeer. She certainly didn't need Logan leaning over her shoulder to offer a seductive "Need any help?"

"No, thanks." She was pleased to hear how calm her voice sounded. Slipping a small makeup bag from her purse, she took out a compact and briefly studied her reflection before dabbing an extra layer of powder on her nose. Then she added a tad more to her forehead and chin for good measure.

"There, is that better?" she demanded of the cameraman.

Logan took it upon himself to answer, "Not quite." He took the compact from Marnie's hands and set about stroking the sable brush over her cheekbones. Shivers ran down her spine, curling her toes. Who would ever have guessed that a simple makeup brush could become a powerful tool of seduction?

"Pucker up," he ordered huskily.

"What!" Marnie sent a rapid glance to the cameraman to see if he'd overheard Logan's outrageous suggestion. Luckily Joe was adjusting the video camera's shoulder mount and appeared to be unaware of what was going on between Logan and Marnie.

Logan held a pot of lip gloss which he must have taken out of the makeup bag without her noticing.

"Pucker up," he repeated, dabbing a lip brush into the gloss.

"I don't—"

"Perfect." He complimented her as her lips unintentionally took on the shape he'd requested.

Marnie was afraid to move for fear she'd end up with a slash of lip gloss across her cheek. Her eyes more than made up for her verbal silence, however, and flashed their anger to Logan in no uncertain terms. He was turning this interview into a three-ring circus. *No, scratch that,* she decided as he put the lip brush aside to carry on with his fingertip. *Not a circus, but a cinematic seduction scene!*

She resisted the unprofessional temptation to bite the finger that was flirtatiously taunting her mouth, and fixed him with a look of calm tolerance, which worked so well with disruptive patients.

Apparently it also worked on Logan. He stopped his provocative actions and wiped his fingers with a Kleenex he snitched from the box on her desk. Under the pretext of slipping her makeup bag back into her purse, he leaned close enough to whisper, "Actually I prefer the natural look myself."

"That's much better." Joe gave his enthusiastic approval, unaware of the sexual overtones of their exchange.

"Fine." Her voice was a study of enforced patience. "What's next?"

"Logan will wire you for sound," Joe replied.

Marnie didn't like the sound of that, and her unease increased when Logan grinned and ordered her to take off her jacket.

"What for?" she demanded.

"So I can arrange your microphone." The gleam in his eyes told her that the microphone wasn't the only thing he was thinking of arranging. "Come on, this won't hurt."

There was nothing Marnie could do but reluctantly obey his command. Logan certainly made the most of the situation, leisurely uncoiling the wire so that it climbed up her back. As he did so, his investigative fingers made note of the fact that beneath her blouse she was wearing a smooth chemise rather than a bra.

Marnie bit her tongue and looked straight ahead, concentrating doggedly on the small print of her degree hanging on the wall across from where she sat.

Logan deliberately chose to have the audio wire follow a provocative route, positioning it under, rather than over, the top of her arm. When his fingertips inevitably came into contact with the side of her breast, he murmured a teasing "Pardon me."

"Never in a million years," she murmured back, barely moving her lips.

Seeing that he'd pushed his luck far enough, he instructed her to put her jacket back on. Once she'd done so, he efficiently clipped the tiny microphone onto her lapel.

"Do we start filming now?" Her question was voiced in the tone of one holding on to her temper with the greatest of difficulty.

"Whenever Logan's ready," Joe answered.

"Logan's been *ready* since he first met you," Logan muttered for her ears only.

He then had the effrontery to amble on over to the other side of the desk to begin his lead-in as if nothing had passed between them.

Before he could get to his first question, however, Joe cut in with an urgent "Hold it, I've got some trouble here." He carefully lowered the camera to a nearby chair and slipped the battery pack from across his shoulder.

"What's wrong?" Now Logan seemed all business.

Joe growled a few muttered curses. "The rain must have gotten into the battery pack. I'll have to go back down to the van to get another one to see if that'll work."

"We'll wait here for you," Logan said.

The moment Joe was out the door, Marnie gave vent to her feelings. "I don't appreciate the fun you're having at my expense."

Crossing his arms over his chest, Logan innocently asked, "And what fun might that be?"

"You know exactly what I'm talking about. The verbal baiting, the sexual innuendos."

79

"That's the trouble with you shrinks." He shook his head at her. "You're always reading something into nothing. You need to loosen up, Dr. Lathrope. You're much too tense." He took up a position directly behind her chair. His hands settled on her shoulders, and his thumbs performed a circular dance on her upper back. "Just feel these muscles. Tight as a drum." He clicked his tongue in disapproval. "Relax."

Relax? Marnie said to herself. An impossible suggestion where Logan was concerned. She could never relax her guard around him!

CHAPTER FIVE

"You're going to dislodge my microphone!" Marnie protested as Logan's back rub became more daring.

"You've already dislodged my peace of mind," he murmured, running an index finger along the bare curve of her neck. "And I personally promise to repair anything I dislodge."

"Oh, no, you don't." Marnie sat stiffly erect. "You're not wiring me for sound again. Once was more than enough."

"Spoilsport."

"Damn right. We're here to do a serious interview on a major social problem, not to fool around!"

"You're absolutely right." Logan astounded her by agreeing.

"Good. I'm glad you see my point," she said as he moved away.

Logan nodded, his expression sagaciously solemn. "We'll do the interview first and *then* we'll fool around."

A clinical psychologist must be tactful, patient, and able to deal with difficult people in a firm but sympathetic manner, Marnie silently recited. *Remember that!*

Joe's return prevented Logan from teasing Marnie any further.

"It'll just take me a second to hook this back up and then we'll be rolling," Joe promised.

Marnie's guardian angel finally came to bat for her, and the interview proceeded without any further complications. Logan's questions were direct and to the point. Marnie strove

81

to make her answers equally so.

Logan began by asking, "What makes a man beat his wife?"

"Family violence is usually a learned pattern of behavior. A batterer often comes from a home where he was abused as a child or where he saw his mother being abused. He learns that violence is the way one deals with conflicts and emotions."

"Why do women put up with it?"

"Lack of financial resources, hope that their husbands will change, fear of the unknown, fear of retaliation should they leave. I want to make one thing clear, however. Although some women *tolerate* violence, that's not to say that they *invite* it, or *enjoy* it," Marnie stressed. "The implication that they do is one of three major misconceptions about wife abuse."

"What are the other two major misconceptions?"

"That wife abuse primarily occurs among low-income groups. Untrue. Wife abuse cuts across all ethnic, racial, and socioeconomic lines. The third misconception concerns alcohol, which is commonly blamed for spousal violence. Alcohol and drugs can trigger violent behavior, as can job-related stresses. But they are not the cause of the violence."

"How widespread is the problem?"

"Marital abuse has been called the silent crime. Consequently statistics are hard to come by, because often the crime is not reported," Marnie explained. "However, it's estimated that nearly six million women are physically abused by their husbands or boyfriends in any one year, and that half of all women are beaten by their husbands at least once in their married lives. According to an FBI report, forty-one percent of the women murdered in this country are killed by their husbands."

"What can be done to help solve the plight of battered women?"

"Short-term help can be found at shelters, such as the Safe Place, which will be opening soon here in Charleston. But we need more shelters of that type. The ultimate solution lies in preventing physical abuse in the first place. Prevention starts with people changing their attitudes toward violence and women. No one deserves to be beaten or physically threatened, no matter what the excuse. It's a crime to beat anyone—a stranger, your friend, or your wife—and the law should be enforced. Our society needs to stop tolerating violence as a means of resolving conflict and expressing anger. Only then can we have men and women capable of dealing with each other with equality and mutual respect."

Logan waited a moment and then gestured to Joe. "That's a wrap."

Joe nodded and stopped filming. "Since we had some technical problems, I'm going to take this tape on down to the van and replay it; make sure it looks good."

"Fine. I'll be down in a few minutes," Logan told him. Once Joe left, Logan switched off the quartz lights and returned the room to its former restfulness. "I think the interview went well, all things considered."

Marnie blinked as her eyes adjusted to the sudden change in light. "What things?"

"I was weaving sexual fantasies around you," Logan confessed with intended provocativeness.

Marnie decided it was time to fight fire with fire. "Really?" she purred. "That makes two of us."

Logan almost dropped the stick of gum he was about to unwrap. "What?"

"Women have sexual fantasies too. You told me so yourself," she reminded him. "It's not at all unusual for a woman to fantasize about a man's body in much the same way a man fantasizes about a woman's body."

"Wait a minute here!" He waved the foil-wrapped stick of gum through the air. "Are you telling me that while you were sitting there at your desk, all cool and professional, you were actually—"

"Admiring your tush," she readily inserted. "Why the shocked look, Logan? Surely you've been complimented before on that part of your anatomy." The pert remark was accompanied by the feminine version of a leer.

Logan eyed her warily, as if unsure of her intentions. "What is this, a lesson in role reversals?"

"How astute of you." Her tone was congratulatory.

Logan mockingly clutched his hand to his heart. "How can you play such a cruel trick on a man already driven to the ragged edge by a lack of nicotine and feminine companionship?"

Lack of feminine companionship? She doubted that. As for the nicotine . . . "How have things been going without cigarettes?" Marnie felt remiss at not having asked him about that earlier.

"The guys are embarrassed to go out to coffee with me," he announced with a grin.

"Why?"

"I find myself gnawing on those plastic stirring sticks that come with Styrofoam cups. And I'm sure I've added substantially to the fortunes of the makers of Wrigley's chewing gum. I'm already up to two packs a day." He finished unwrapping the gum and popped it into his mouth.

Marnie smiled at his humor. "Physically, how are you feeling?"

"Occasionally jumpy," he ruefully acknowledged, "but otherwise pretty good."

"It's been ten days now. I've heard the first week is the worst."

"That's encouraging. A buddy of mine said that the first year or two was the worst. Then the next six or seven years weren't quite so bad. With moral support like that, who needs enemies, right?"

"I'm sure he was just trying to be helpful."

"That's true. He is the one who warned me to seek help should I find myself sniffing my fingers for any lingering scents of nicotine."

"Sounds like good advice to me," Marnie agreed with a laugh.

Joe returned to the office just then with the good news that the tape looked excellent. "You can take the mike off now, Dr. Lathrope," he told Marnie.

"Allow me," Logan offered, rushing forward with a devilish gleam in his sherry-colored eyes.

Marnie held out her hand in an excellent imitation of a traffic cop. "Hold it right there. I'm sure I can manage this on my own. Shouldn't you be helping Joe with the equipment or something?"

Logan slowed his forward movement until he came to a halt right beside the chair where she sat. Marnie's eyes were on the level of his fourth shirt button. She watched the third and then the second button come into view as he hunkered down until he was looking directly into her eyes.

"I am helping Joe with something," he calmly informed her. "This equipment is entrusted to our care, and we can't have anything happening to it."

Marnie cast her eyes heavenward and took a deep sigh. A moment later she sincerely wished she hadn't, for the lace inset of her blouse managed to get snagged on the clip of the microphone.

"Now you've done it." Logan's accusation was spoken in a stage whisper. His fingers immediately homed in on the troubled area, directly atop her right breast.

Marnie wrapped surprisingly strong fingers around his wrist and said, "If I might make a suggestion? Why don't you just have Diane come in here to help me while you and Joe go take a hike."

Logan regretfully agreed. "If you insist."

"I do."

Marnie didn't breathe comfortably again until Diane slipped into the office in the wake of the departing men.

"I'll be back . . ." Logan promised right before closing the door. "For the microphone." His expressive eyes told her that wasn't all he was coming back for.

Diane watched with grinning approval as Logan carefully shut the door behind him. "Whatta tush!" she declared half under her breath, unknowingly repeating Marnie's teasing observation. "Whatta body!"

"Diane, if you don't mind. I could use some help here." Marnie's voice was sharper than normal.

"Oh, sure. Sorry." Diane hastened to her side and quickly untangled the microphone clip from the seductive lace of Marnie's blouse.

"Thanks." Marnie viewed, with marked dislike, the snake-like coil of audio wire now lying on her desk.

"Everybody else has gone home for the day," Diane told her.

For the first time since Logan's arrival at four, Marnie glanced at her watch. It was almost six! "Thanks for staying, Diane. You can go now. I'll lock up."

"I've got a date tonight or I'd stay. Not that it would do me any good. I saw the way Logan was looking at you."

Marnie had seen it too. Seen it and wondered what she was going to do about it.

"Aren't you warm in that suit of yours?" Logan questioned

Marnie upon his return. Diane had already gone home. "It is the end of June, you know, not January."

"How kind of you to be so concerned about my comfort, Logan."

"Your comfort isn't the only thing I'm concerned about," he murmured.

I'm sure it isn't, she thought to herself, imagining any number of possible provocative answers he might come up with. None of them proved to be accurate because Logan surprised her by, saying, "I'm concerned about what's going on between us."

"So am I," she admitted quietly.

"For different reasons, I fear," he stated wryly. "I'm concerned that I'm *not* getting anywhere with you, while you're no doubt concerned that I *am.*"

"Why don't you ever talk about your past?" Marnie suddenly asked.

Logan's expression mirrored his surprise. "You do have this disconcerting habit of tossing questions out of left field."

"Perhaps if I knew more about you I wouldn't be so wary of you," Marnie said by way of explanation.

"There's no need to be wary of me," he huskily assured her.

"Then tell me about yourself."

He shied away from her quiet request. "I'm thirty-one, single, and gainfully employed. What else do you need to know?"

"Your driver's license could have told me that much," she retorted. "I'd like to know more about the kind of man you are."

"The kind who wants you."

Marnie shook her head at his seductive words. "I'd really like to know, Logan." Her voice was direct.

"Then come to dinner with me."

She was disappointed by his continued avoidance, and it showed in her mocking inflection: "Sure. All I have to do is go to dinner with you, and you'll tell me all about yourself, right?"

"Right."

"Bull!" she stated bluntly. "You'll just continue sidestepping the issue as you have since I first met you." She shook her head in exasperation. "Logan, how can we examine the possibility of becoming involved in a relationship when you won't be honest with me?"

"All right." He shoved a restless hand through his dark hair. "We'll talk. But not here. Not in your office with you playing shrink."

"Fair enough," she agreed. "But not in some romantic restaurant either. We need some kind of neutral territory."

"How about Charles Towne Landing," he suggested, naming Charleston's innovative nature preserve and permanent historical site. "We could go for an old-fashioned picnic on the Fourth of July. I've got to be out of town until then anyway."

The news of his departure came as a complete surprise to Marnie. "What about the rest of the series on battered women? When are you going to speak to Gwen Davis and the other members of the Women's Coalition?"

"When I get back next week."

She couldn't resist the temptation of asking, "Is your trip business or pleasure?"

"Business," he answered, albeit briefly. "What about the picnic idea? Is it a date?"

She stared at him intently for a moment, almost as if hoping to see the truth of his thoughts. "You are serious about talking? No subterfuge?"

"Cross my heart." He suited his actions to his pledge. "There is one hitch, however."

"I knew there had to be at least one." There was a certain sarcasm in her sigh as she gathered her belongings. "What is it?"

"That I pick you up at your house. No more of this separate-car routine."

"All right," she agreed, without any argument. "You can pick me up at about eleven in the morning, if that's okay for you?"

"Eleven sounds fine." Logan stepped aside so she could lock the office door.

"I'll bring the food," she said as they walked past the outer office reception area.

Logan looked surprised. "You don't have to do that."

Marnie locked the main office door before saying, "I know I don't have to, which is why I'd like to."

"Sounds like a good reason to me," he said approvingly. "Same reason I've got for walking you to your car. That, plus the fact that I'm aching to kiss you," he huskily tacked on seconds before the elevator door parted to admit them into its crowded confines.

Anticipation accelerated Marnie's breathing and pulse all the way to the parking lot. She unlocked her car door and managed to stow her briefcase and purse into the front seat without mishap. Turning to face Logan, she took a deep breath—only to have his mouth swoop down to steal it from hers.

The kiss lingered in Marnie's mind throughout the days and especially the nights that Logan was out of town. She heard nothing from him during the week between the interview and Independence Day. Logan merely appeared at her house at eleven on the morning of July Fourth.

Rand, who was taking advantage of the clear and unexpectedly cool weather to sand the wrought-iron railing of the gate guarding the driveway, was the first to greet Logan. Marnie watched the two men from her third-floor window.

They were still deep in conversation when she joined them a few minutes later, wicker picnic basket in hand.

"You look lovely, Scarlett," Logan stated softly. As he took the hamper from her, his fingers deliberately lingered on hers. His eyes likewise lingered on the stunning picture she made.

Marnie had had second thoughts about wearing the wide-brimmed straw hat, but her reasons for keeping it on were practical. As a redhead, she was sensitive to the sun and needed the protection the hat provided. Besides, it went well with her flower-sprigged sundress with the wide sash and generously full skirt that swung against her bare legs. Her leather sandals had already proven their worth in comfort. Since they planned on spending a good deal of the day outside, she'd opted for coolness and so had gathered her hair up and secured it with a gold hair clasp in a variation of a ponytail, which was tucked into the crown of her hat.

"I see you two have met," she said, feeling unaccountably nervous.

Rand gave her a nod that said he approved of her choice of companion for the day.

"We'd better get going," Logan stated. "It was nice meeting you, Rand."

"Same here," Rand returned. "Have a great time."

And they did. The park was located about three miles northwest of downtown Charleston, so the drive was short. It was a beautiful day, full of sunshine and the sweet smell of summer flowers.

After helping her out of the Datsun, Logan asked, "Shall we eat first?"

"Sounds good to me."

"What do you have in here?" He groaned as he lifted the picnic hamper from the Datsun's hatchback.

"Goodies."

They selected a picnic table away from the others, with a view of a serene pond graced with ducks. Marnie flipped up the hamper's lid and brought out a paper tablecloth.

"You've got to be kidding." Logan laughed. "A table-cloth?"

"Why not? There's no way of knowing what little critters had been cavorting across this table before we got here."

"Now that you put it that way, a tablecloth sounds like a good idea," Logan judiciously agreed.

"Good, then you can lay it out." Marnie lifted the hamper onto the wooden seat to temporarily get it out of his way.

"Speaking of little critters, I'd like to stop by the natural habitat zoo they've got here. I've never been there."

"Neither have I," Marnie admitted. "In fact, this is the first time I've been here at all."

"Really?" Logan sounded as if he found that hard to believe. "It's one of my favorite places in the city. I guess it must be because of all the wide-open space here. It doesn't feel hemmed in." He seemed almost nostalgic.

"I imagine Charleston must be quite different from Montana."

"Definitely." He gave the tablecloth a final pat before demanding, "Where's the food?"

She tossed him a teasing look. "Not hungry by any chance, are you?"

"Scarlett, I'm always hungry whenever I'm with you." He stroked her wrist as he took a bag of potato chips from her.

"You should know that by now."

Marnie ruefully shook her head at him and directed her attention to unpacking the rest of the food: her famous guacamole dip, deviled eggs, three-bean salad, plenty of thinly sliced ham, seedless grapes, chilled slices of watermelon, and a large Thermos of sun-brewed iced tea.

"It looks like you've prepared a real feast here," Logan said approvingly. "We used to have spreads like this when I was a kid."

On the verge of munching on a guacamole-laden potato chip, Marnie paused to say, "That's the first time you've ever referred to your childhood."

Logan shrugged nonchalantly. "I don't talk about it much."

"Why not?"

"There you go again," he said, as if to chastise her. "Getting that shrink's gleam in your eye."

"And there you go again, getting defensive and changing the subject," she retorted. "You said we were going to talk."

"Okay, we'll talk. But I'm sure you're going to be disappointed."

"Why do you say that?"

"My past isn't as fertile a source of information about me as you seem to think it will be. In fact, it's downright boring." Logan took a bite of salad before continuing: "I grew up in western Montana, in a little town that isn't even on most maps. My father was a logger, my mom a housewife. I've got two sisters; one older, one younger. Both are married to loggers and both live near my folks. My dad's a foreman now and is talking about retiring. That's it." He flipped his hand, a gesture clearly indicating there was no more to be said on the subject.

"If your past is as uncomplicated as you make out, then

why are you so reluctant to talk about it?"

"Put it down to natural reticence on my part," Logan modestly suggested.

Marnie saw through his teasing defenses and gently pressed him for an answer: "What's the real reason?"

Logan's expression became somber, and his attention drifted to the nearby reflecting pond. "Have you ever felt like a fish out of water?" he asked her softly.

"Sometimes."

"I felt like that a lot as a kid." His eyes remained absently fixed on the pond. "Everyone in my hometown seemed satisfied with their lives. Not me. I longed to get out. I left the day after I finished high school. I knew there was a big world outside of Montana, and I was just itching to see all of it."

"Were you able to see it all?"

"Not all, but a great deal. I took a year off after college and bummed around Europe and the Orient. One year stretched into two. When I finally came back, I got a job working for a small station in Oklahoma. From there I eventually ended up in Phoenix, but I wasn't happy with the station management. The news director here in Charleston viewed one of the résumé tapes I sent out, and offered me *carte blanche* here."

"You can't have been in Charleston very long." At his frowning look of inquiry, she went on to explain. "You haven't picked up a southern drawl yet."

"I've been here almost two years," he said; and hearing that, she was surprised.

"Your parents must be very proud of your success."

Logan's face suddenly became shuttered at her words. His gaze drifted off to the stands of live oaks surrounding the picnic area. "My parents have a hard time accepting what I do for a living. They never understood why I felt compelled to leave in the first place. I get tired of constantly having to defend myself and my profession to my family." His eyes swung back to her attentive face. "It's ironic, then, isn't it, that I get tied up with a woman who also disapproves of television journalists." With a shake of his head, he delivered a mocking diagnosis: "Must be a masochistic streak I've got."

"Logan, it isn't a matter of my disapproving of what you do. I'm concerned about the power the media wield and the far-reaching consequences of that power, but I don't disapprove." Her drawl softened her assurances, which were spoken with a lilting cadence.

"No?" He squinted against the increasing glare of the noonday sun and slipped on his sunglasses. "I seem to recall the term 'glitzy TV personality' being applied."

"I spoke out of anger, not disapproval," she explained. "The fact is that although you may look glitzy in those shades of yours"—she teasingly pushed them further up the bridge of his nose—"you're actually pretty down-to-earth."

"Ah!" He captured her fingers and pressed a kiss to the back of her hand with unexpectedly Continental flair. "A compliment at last. Let's celebrate!"

And so they did, beginning with an exploratory walk through the zoo after their meal. In keeping with the park's historical heritage, the animals there were all those that the original settlers would have seen. Marnie was surprised to find bears and bison roaming in the shady forested area. The animals themselves weren't in cages; instead the visitors walked along enclosed pathways.

From the park they drove on to participate in a host of special activities celebrating America's birthday. Marnie took her first ride in a hot-air balloon, Logan came in second at a watermelon-eating contest, and they both applauded a twilight fireworks display.

By late evening Marnie was feeling pleasantly exhausted after the whirlwind of activity. "I had a wonderful time today," she told Logan as he pulled the Datsun into the driveway, past Rand's newly painted wrought-iron gates.

Logan switched off the car's engine and softly murmured, "Aren't you going to invite me up?"

"I don't have any coffee," she said with a teasing lilt.

"Coffee isn't what I want."

"Logan, I . . ."

"Whatever you have will be fine." His voice was softly persuasive.

They were no longer talking about beverages. In his own way Logan was telling her that whatever happened in her apartment would do so at her pace.

Marnie escalated that pace by unintentionally bumping into Logan as she showed him into her apartment. The place was bathed in darkness, and she'd been reaching for the wall switch to turn on a light when her hand instead collided with the wall of Logan's chest. The contact, slight though it may have been, was enough to send rockets shooting through her. A husky masculine groan and a soft feminine sigh later, their two shadows merged into one.

Marnie reveled in the feel of his warm vibrant body pressed against the entire length of hers. Her heart soared with the indisputable knowledge that this was what she'd been waiting for all day. Exciting though her fun-filled day may have been, it couldn't hold a candle to the raw exhilaration she experienced in his arms.

Those same arms tightened their hold on her, his seeking fingers sliding from her shoulders to the small of her back. Marnie's gasp of pleasure was shared by Logan as she leaned into him, her firm breasts thrusting invitingly against his chest. Pleasure sizzled from the sensitive tips of her breasts down to the aching cradle of her femininity where his hips were moving against hers with an unmistakable intent.

Marnie tilted back her head and waited for the kiss she was sure would follow. She was not disappointed. Logan's mouth descended upon hers with unerring accuracy. Their lips merged and parted, merged and parted, each time with heightened expectation.

His kisses did not remain strictly limited to her mouth but were generously scattered over her cheeks and temples, eyelids and earlobes as well. Yet it was to the sweetness of her parted lips that he again and again returned, drinking of their nectar as if to relieve an unquenchable thirst. Her fingers buried themselves in the rich thickness of his hair as one kiss blended into another and blossomed into an intimate exchange involving penetrating flicks of his tongue that she met with imaginatively provocative moves of her own.

Marnie welcomed the increased intimacy of their embrace as his knee nudged its way between hers. The full skirt of her sundress swirled around the rock-hard muscles of his denim-clad thighs. Her body's increased pliancy indicated her rapidly dwindling self-control. Her hands stroked their way down his spine to the waistband of his jeans where her fingers daringly slipped between the rough denim and the smooth cotton of his shirt. Reflexively she clenched fistfuls of his shirt, her hands kneading him with the sensual contentment of a cat.

Logan's widened stance made the concealment of his growing arousal impossible. His fingers sought and conquered the intricacies of her back-fastened sundress, freeing the straps and slipping them from her shoulders. Only his reluctance to let her move even a centimeter away from him prevented her dress from slipping to her waist. Although in front the material remained a modest shield between them, in the back it gaped wide open, inviting further exploration.

Logan eagerly took advantage of the opportunity to introduce his touch to the satiny softness of her newly revealed flesh. His fingers grazed her shoulder blades and caressed the vulnerable base of her neck before sliding down the valley of her spine and expediently dealing with the confining band of her bra. Now his exploratory mission was free to continue.

He caressed her with long, hypnotic strokes that started at the nape of her neck and ended at the lacy elastic waistband of her silky panties. His touch was unhurried and skillful as he paused to trace a seductive message low down on the small of her back. Deep-seated nerve endings jumped into life to hum with tingling pleasure, blinding Marnie to the danger of prolonging the embrace, until the sudden peal of a ringing telephone brought her back to awareness.

"Let the answering machine get it," Logan muttered against her bare shoulder.

"I can't." Her voice was a husky whisper as she slid the straps of her sundress back up to her shoulders. "It could be important. I'm a doctor, Logan. I have to be available to my patients."

With a muffled groan he reluctantly set her free.

Marnie switched the lights on, and the answering machine off, before snatching up the phone receiver with a shaking hand. "Hello?"

"Marnie? Thank goodness I've finally reached you," Gwen Davis exclaimed.

Marnie inhaled sharply as Logan slid an impudent finger down her still-bare back. Much to his disappointment, she immediately lodged the phone between her ear and shoulder and efficiently redid the fastenings Logan had undone. "What's wrong?"

"Ready or not, we've got our first resident," Gwen answered. "And, Marnie, she needs your help."

Logan watched Marnie's expression sober as she quietly promised, "I'll be right over."

CHAPTER SIX

"Where are you going?" Logan demanded as Marnie hung up the phone and headed out of the room.

"To change," she offered from behind the now closed bedroom door. With a speed that Logan found surprising, she reappeared a few minutes later dressed in a crisp pair of jeans and a navy polo shirt. "I'm afraid I've got to go see a patient."

Logan had a gut feeling that this patient was a battered woman, but he knew better than to question Marnie about it. "You . . . be careful," he instructed her, tenderly caressing the tip of her nose.

Marnie's warm smile silently thanked him for not asking any of the questions she could see written in his eyes. "I will."

He did allow himself one emphatic request, however. "Call me when you get back home."

"I can't do that. It will probably be very late," Marnie replied as she checked to make sure she had her keys.

"That doesn't matter. I'm sure I'll be awake." As Logan followed Marnie down the well-lit staircase, he couldn't help but admire the decidedly feminine curve of her denim-clad bottom. It was the first time he'd seen her in pants, he realized. He'd seen a lot of women with sexy figures wearing well-fitted designer jeans, but none of them had ever affected him as strongly as this woman did in a simple pair of Levi jeans. "Yes, I'm sure I'll be awake," he repeated, wryly adding, "Probably spending my time standing under a cold shower."

Marnie spent most of the night talking and, even more important, *listening* to a woman who'd snuck out of her house with her two small children after her abusive husband had gone out.

"He beat me this time for overcooking his steak," Pam Parker told Marnie in the toneless voice that accompanied shock. The woman's lips were cut and swollen, as was her right eye. "Last time it was because the car wouldn't start."

"Those are just excuses he uses to try to justify beating you," Marnie gently responded. "The truth is that none of your actions really cause your husband's violent behavior. It comes from within *him*. I'd like you to try and remember that. You haven't done anything wrong, this isn't your fault."

Pam blinked back tears. "It isn't?"

"No, it isn't."

"I had to go see my doctor the last time . . . the last time my husband beat me. I was afraid he'd broken my rib, so I had to go, you know?" Pam wiped away her tears and gratefully clenched the comforting hand Marnie offered. "The first question my doctor asked me was what had I done to make my husband beat me."

"And by asking that, the doctor immediately put the blame on you, right?"

Pam nodded. "I tried to cook better meals, to keep the house cleaner. It didn't make any difference."

"Of course it didn't. Because you were never the real reason for your husband's violent behavior. You were the excuse. Can you see the difference?"

Again Pam nodded. "It wasn't my fault?"

Marnie repeated her assurance. "It wasn't your fault." She was well aware that one of the most important ways she could offer help was to mitigate the battered woman's sense of guilt. "No more than it's a victim's fault that he was mugged."

The analogy appeared to be one Pam could identify with. "Thanks, Dr. Lathrope."

"Call me Marnie," she said. Marnie felt Pam and the other women like her were not so much patients as they were friends in need of help.

Marnie let herself into her apartment at two thirty that night. She checked the messages on her answering machine, none of which were urgent, and debated over calling Logan.

As if operating on some sixth sense, Logan phoned at that very moment. "You're home." He sounded relieved.

"I just got in."

"How're you doing?" he asked, his voice husky with concern.

"Okay. How about you?"

"I've used up all the cold water in the house, but it doesn't seem to have helped. What should I do, Doctor?"

Logan's teasing use of her professional title reminded her of the night he'd admitted his nervousness over giving up cigarettes, and she spoke her thoughts aloud: "I'm very proud of you, you know."

"No, I didn't know. Thanks, but what brought that up?"

"The fact that you're winning the battle against smoking," she answered.

To which Logan seductively asked, "Am I also winning your affection?"

Marnie didn't know whether it was a result of the early morning hour or Logan's persuasive voice, but she found herself abandoning her fortified caution and taking a risk. "Yes, you're also winning my affection." Her honest response was as seductive as Logan's question had been.

His muffled groan carried clearly over the phone lines. "Now she tells me, when I'm too far away to kiss her."

"I wouldn't worry about it," she softly returned. "My

head's still reeling from the last kiss we shared."

"Did I tell you how incredibly soft your skin is? Or how good you feel against me? Scarlett, you fit me just right."

Marnie's breathing deepened. There was something erotic about hearing such intimate compliments over the phone in the dead of night. "You're making me blush."

"All over?"

"Yes, all over."

Logan groaned again and made a rueful accusation: "I'm not going to be able to sleep now, you know that, don't you?"

"Try closing your eyes and counting sheep."

He could hear the smile in her voice. "I'd rather close my eyes and imagine you lying here beside me in my bed."

"Logan . . ." Now it was Marnie's turn to stifle a hungry sigh. "I've got to get up early in the morning."

"I know. Sweet dreams, Scarlett."

Her dreams were not only sweet, they were sensual.

Pam Parker's arrival marked the real beginning of the shelter. Logan kept his promise and interviewed Gwen Davis and several other members of the Women's Coalition, reluctantly accepting the proviso that the shelter itself was off-limits.

"Why this cloak-and-dagger routine about even the general location of the shelter?" Logan questioned Gwen at their first meeting in one of Charleston's numerous public parks. He felt more like a CIA agent than a television journalist. "How do you expect people seeking your help to find you?"

"People in need will have no trouble finding us," Gwen replied. "Most of our residents will be referred to us by other social agencies. As for the location of the shelter itself, that will change periodically. Having roving shelters has become necessary in some cases for security reasons. Some shelters are able to afford expensive security systems, but we haven't reached that stage yet. We do hope eventually to keep the shelter in one permanent location, but until that time we will have to rotate sites."

"When you say it's necessary for security reasons, what exactly are you referring to?"

"It's imperative that a woman have the time away from her husband to sort out her options. She can't do that if her husband knows where she is, and makes demands, either verbal or physical, for her return. And angry husbands have been known to vandalize or otherwise attack shelters in an angry rage."

"Great, just great!" Logan muttered, restlessly pulling out a pack of gum. His fears about Marnie's safety were well-founded.

Gwen looked at him warily. "I beg your pardon?"

"Don't you worry about your safety?"

"We are extremely careful, and we're working on improving the cooperation of the local police force in responding to an emergency, should one arise. However, I'd rather we returned to the subject of the shelter itself rather than dwelling on security measures," Gwen stated firmly.

Logan had difficulty getting his mind off Marnie's safety, but his professionalism came to the fore as he efficiently questioned Gwen about the shelter's services and the need for more of such refuges. He ended by asking, "What will the shelter be called?"

"The Safe Place."

He certainly hoped it would be safe—safe for Marnie.

Logan's special report on battered women aired in mid-August. From that day forward the fifteen-bed shelter was constantly full. Bunk beds and infant cribs were crammed into almost every available nook and cranny of what had formerly been a large two-story home. The Safe Place had sufficient funding to afford only two full-time employees, one administrator for days and one for nights. Someone was needed part-time to fill in on weekends. Consequently Marnie spent numerous weekends and evenings offering her assistance.

Marnie was well aware of Logan's concerns for her safety. He brought the subject up whenever they were together, which wasn't as often as either one would have liked. The heavy demands on Marnie's time continued as the sizzling heat of August gave way to the slightly cooler temperatures of September.

"You've been working too hard," Logan told Marnie, who was sitting beside him on her couch one rainy Sunday evening.

"Things have been pretty hectic lately." She shifted her head into a more comfortable position against his shoulder. "Did I tell you that Elaine's designed several play projects to involve the children, and several churches have donated boxes of toys for them? We've also received donations of clothing, and it looks like we might finally get another window air conditioner. Gwen says the funding situation is looking up, and for that we owe a great deal to your series."

"Still think television journalists are a glitzy lot?" he asked her.

"Unh, unh." Marnie placed a sleepy kiss on his chin. "You're wonderful and your series was wonderful."

Logan spread massaging fingers through hair like molten silk. "You know what you need?"

"About twelve hours of uninterrupted sleep," she replied groggily, covering a yawn.

"In addition to that." He directed his attention to soothing the tense muscles of her neck. "You need a day off, a day away from it all. You've worked practically every weekend this month. Look at this weekend; you were at the shelter all day yesterday and most of today. It's time you took at least a Saturday off."

Marnie knew Logan was right. She had been overworking. "How about next Saturday?" she said.

"Perfect. We could take a drive up the coast and spend the day along the Grand Strand," he suggested, naming South Carolina's famous fifty-five-mile stretch of coastal beaches. "How does that sound?"

"Lovely."

"It will be," he promised with a smoldering look that told her his patience was coming to an end.

Since the night of the Fourth of July when they'd been interrupted, they had shared many such embraces—and a growing intimacy. Marnie no longer bothered denying her feelings for Logan, although she had yet to identify them as love. Whatever this was between them, the feeling was too strong to fight, and too good to pass up. As a precautionary measure she'd renewed her prescription for the pill. But going to bed with Logan called for an emotional commitment on her part, a commitment she didn't want to make until she was sure.

Saturday brought with it the promise of a warm Indian-summer day. Marnie had chosen her outfit with care. Her khaki trousers were stylish yet comfortable, and the matching cotton-knit top presented a striking contrast to her red hair.

The leisurely two-hour drive north from Charleston was intended to be made without any stops. But that was before Marnie caught sight of a garish sign.

"Look," she exclaimed. "There's a flea market! Let's stop."

Logan turned off Highway 17 onto the open field that, for

the day, had been transformed into a bargain bazaar. He managed to squeeze the Datsun into the only available parking space, between two pickup trucks.

Logan had long since repaired the passenger-door handle, so that Marnie was able to open her own door. He still made a point of assisting her up from the low-slung seat, however, and never resisted the opportunity to tug her right into his arms and then quickly release her. Even then, Logan kept his fingers threaded through Marnie's as they strolled amid the browsing crowds of people.

Card tables and picnic tables were strewn with varying collections of goodies, from paperback books and old records to fine china and costume jewelry. While Logan studied a collection of campaign buttons from the past fifty years, Marnie moved on to the next table, which held a promising array of clothing. Her curiosity paid off when she came across a pile of full-length cotton nightgowns from the early twenties. The original price tags were still stapled to the fronts: Dinkerman's Dry Goods—25¢.

Allowing for inflation, the current vendor was asking a dollar for the hand-embroidered sleepwear. Marnie fell in love with the entire pile immediately and snatched up all four nightgowns with eager hands. Each was in a different pastel color: pink, lilac, yellow, and blue, with contrasting embroidery.

Caught up in her streak of good luck, she started guiltily when Logan approached her from behind and asked, "What've you got there?"

"Nightgowns."

His eyebrows arched above his familiar sunglasses. "Sexy?"

"I'm not interested in whether or not they're sexy," she informed him before pulling out her wallet and trying to gain

106

the busy vendor's attention.

"Maybe not, but I am." Being several inches taller than she, Logan was easily able to lean over her shoulder to peruse her intended purchase. "They don't look very sexy to me."

"That's because you have no imagination," she retorted.

"Oh, I wouldn't say that," he drawled, running his index finger down the side of her cheek.

The harried vendor finally attended to Marnie and said, "That'll be four dollars."

She handed over a five-dollar bill.

"Would you like a bag for those?" the woman asked as she gave Marnie her change.

"Yes, please."

"I hope you enjoy them," the woman added with a pointed glance in Logan's direction.

To Marnie's chagrin, Logan obligingly retorted, "I'm sure *we* will!"

They reached Myrtle Beach, the sun-and-fun capital of the Grand Strand, in time for lunch, only to get bogged down in a minitraffic jam along Ocean Boulevard. The pace of Myrtle Beach's main drag was indeed dragging, but it gave Logan and Marnie both the opportunity to stake out the city's attractions.

"Ever been here in the summer?" Logan asked as they moved forward another few yards, only to be stopped at a red light.

Marnie shook her head. "I decided not to after reading somewhere that the influx of tourists each summer swells Myrtle Beach's usual population of just under twenty thousand to nearly three hundred and fifty thousand."

"Hey, that's great!" Logan exclaimed.

"No, it's not. Two's company, three hundred and fifty thousand is a crowd."

"No, I was talking about the amusement park. I wasn't sure if it would be open today. And look, there's a parking space." He immediately slid the Datsun into the meager opening.

"We're too old for this," she told him a few minutes later as he led her up to the main ticket booth.

"Speak for yourself. Personally, I try and visit the bumper cars at least twice a year," he proudly informed her. "It releases all my pent-up anger toward drivers who steal my parking space or Sunday drivers who go twenty in a fifty-five-mile-an-hour zone." True to his word, after purchasing two entrance tickets, Logan headed straight for the bumper cars.

After a bone-rattling trip on the bumper cars Logan took Marnie over to the shooting gallery, where he shot down a host of metal targets and won her a huge panda bear.

Marnie reciprocated by tossing three beanbags through a center hoop in the next booth and winning her choice of prizes from the first display shelf. She selected a dancing hula doll complete with swiveling hips and paper skirt, which she presented to Logan.

Indicating the native Hawaiian garb, Logan told her, "You'd look good in one of these."

"So would you," she shot back with a ready grin that he just had to kiss.

When, a few minutes later, Logan saw Marnie enviously eyeing a passing cone full of cotton candy, he stopped at the next stand and ordered one for her. She stood by and watched as a sun-bronzed teenager artfully wound the swirling strands of spun sugar around a paper cone. Once the confectionary creation reached a ten-inch diameter, the teenager pulled it out of the machine and presented it to her.

Marnie generously shared her treat with Logan, who much preferred the taste of her sugar-coated mouth to that of the cotton candy. They laughed and kissed like teenagers; even their embrace was youthfully exuberant. Logan's left arm encircled her waist while his right arm encircled the panda bear and Hawaiian doll. In a moment of mischievousness Marnie slowly slid her hand from his waist and snuck her fingers into the back pocket of his white tennis shorts.

They were having a wonderful time until Logan suggested they ride the Tunnel of Doom. Marnie, who loved scary rides, readily agreed. They were strapped into a close relative of a roller-coaster car with safety bars and shipped forward into the pitch-black tunnel. Within ten minutes they were back in the sunlight again, after having endured twisting curves and blind falls, all within unrelieved darkness.

When Marnie's eyes had adjusted to the sunlight, she realized that Logan's face was quite pale. "Are you all right?" she asked.

"Let's get out of here," he demanded somewhat raggedly.

He strode back to the car with rapid steps that had Marnie hurrying to keep up with him. But when they arrived at the car, Logan paused only long enough to toss in their prizes before locking the car again. "I need some air, maybe a walk along the beach."

"Okay," she softly agreed. Obviously something was wrong, but she would wait until Logan was willing to discuss it.

After all the hectic activity of the amusement park, Marnie welcomed the respite provided by the beach. Its wide expanse stretched out in both directions for as far as the eye could see. The temperamental Atlantic rolled in toward the shore, its mood buoyant rather than turbulent. The late-afternoon sun was partially obstructed by the numerous blocks of hotels built along the beach, so the sun worshipers had already packed up their belongings and moved on. That left the hard-packed sand relatively empty for the small groups of shell seekers who avidly combed the tidal waters for treasures.

Logan's pace didn't slow for several minutes, and only then because a breathless Marnie demanded timeout. She sank down onto the cool dry sand without regard for her clothing. Her slacks were replaceable, her exhausted legs were not!

Logan dropped down beside her, his looped arms slung around his bent knees. Not for the first time that day, Marnie admired his tanned legs revealed by his tennis shorts. The muscles of his calves and thighs were firm and muscular. Even his knees were nice and not the least bit knobby.

As Logan showed no sign of wanting to talk, Marnie was content to be quiet. The circling sea gulls became curious about the two still figures and swooped down to see if there was any possibility that a handout could be begged from one of them. They hit the jackpot as Marnie dug out a half-empty bag of pretzels, a leftover from the amusement park that she'd stashed in one of the oversize pockets of her trousers. The gulls trumpeted their approval with raucous cries as one of the more daring of the lot stole an entire pretzel right out of her hand. Logan watched the bird's antics with a smile.

"Do you want to talk about it?"

He shook his head. "Not really, but I suppose I owe you an explanation."

"You don't owe me anything, Logan."

He sighed deeply, not certain where to begin. "That last ride we took reminded me of an . . . unpleasant episode in my life." There was just no fancy way of putting this. For the first time in several weeks Logan truly craved a cigarette. "Do you remember me telling you that I spent a few years traveling abroad?"

"Yes."

Logan didn't like talking about this episode in his life, so his explanation was accordingly brief. "What I didn't tell you was that I spent some time in prison."

"Prison!"

"I was trying to hitchhike my way from Europe, across Turkey, into Asia. The local police thought I looked suspicious, so they tossed me in jail while they searched my belongings and checked my passport."

"But that's illegal!"

"Not in the country I was in. Needless to say, the accommodations weren't exactly the Ritz." Logan's voice hardened as he remembered the darkness of his dank cell, the shuffling of vermin, and the muffled curses of the other prisoners.

The starkness of his expression sent a shiver down Marnie's spine.

With a shake of his head Logan erased the memories. "Anyway, I was lucky. They released me after forty-eight hours and kicked me out of the country."

"Oh, Logan, I'm sorry." She leaned her chin against his shoulder and rubbed a soothing hand down his arm. The thought of him being locked up was intolerable to her. Looking back on the Tunnel of Doom, she could understand why the ride would trigger memories of his incarceration.

Marnie suddenly saw the depth of her feelings for Logan with unexpected clarity. She loved him. She wasn't expecting the realization to hit her with the vividness of the metaphorical lightning bolt, but it did. She loved him. And loving him simplified all the complexities.

She had never felt closer to him than she did at that moment. "I'm glad you've shared this with me."

His hand reached out to clasp hers, his fingers slid between hers. "I want to share more with you. I want to make love to you, I want to have you make love to me."

And there in the mellow twilight of an autumn day on a

public beach, Marnie simply said "Yes."

"I've tried not to rush you, I've been patient," Logan continued before he realized what she'd said. "Yes?"

"Yes." She nodded in confirmation.

"When?"

"Now."

"Here?" He gazed at the sand surrounding them.

She laughingly shook her head. "Not *right* here."

"I think we can find something more private close by." Logan's mouth fastened upon hers, but the contact was brief, as if he no longer trusted his ability to restrain himself, to be satisfied with kissing alone. "Very close by!"

They hurriedly returned to the car, and Logan set off on Ocean Boulevard. Two blocks later he pulled into a sweeping landscaped drive leading to a luxurious hotel. But Marnie could feel the romance of the moment dissolving in the bustling world of reality. She didn't want their first time to be in a hotel, regardless of how ritzy it might be.

"Logan . . ." She stopped him from getting out of the car. "I hate to do this to you . . ."

"You've changed your mind?" The question was gritty with restraint.

"Only about going to a hotel," she hastily assured him. "It's too . . . impersonal. Would you mind if we went back to your place instead?" Logan had rented a beach house on Sullivan's Island that Marnie had taken to the first time he'd shown it to her. "I know it's a two-hour drive back, but . . ."

His voice softened, deepened. "If you'd feel more comfortable at my beach house, we'll go back to my house."

They had to stop for dinner along the way, which added another hour to the return trip. By the time they parked in front of his rented beach house, Logan's needs had progressed beyond the state of readiness to a state of painful arousal.

He didn't even bother turning on the lights when he brought Marnie inside the weathered cedar structure. He simply turned the dead bolt on the front door behind him, swept her up in his arms, and headed for what she presumed to be the bedroom.

Once there Marnie, too, was overcome by this maelstrom of passion. The moment Logan set her on her feet, she kicked off her shoes and set to work on taking his shirt off his muscular torso. Logan's moccasins went the way of her sandals as he whisked her khaki mesh top over her head. Successive layers of clothing were impatiently disposed of: her trousers, his shorts, their underwear.

At last they stood with no barriers between them. Moonlight streamed through the open window and guided Logan's hands over the curves and inlets of her body. His lips fastened on hers with an unleashed hunger that immediately flared out of control and sent them tumbling sideways onto the bed; they landed on the soft mattress with legs and arms intimately entangled.

His hands swirled over the curves of her breasts and fervently caressed their rosy peaks into tautness. Once their arousal was assured, he entrusted their continued seduction to the care of his darting tongue and moved his stimulating fingers to the center of her sexuality. Marnie breathlessly reciprocated. Her tactile voyage of intimate discovery found his velvety strength.

Logan's body was so tightly strung, his fiery passion so aroused, that her feathery touch sent him reeling. His lips returned to hers, stifling her gasp of sensual surprise as with one electrifying thrust he joined them together. Marnie relished the spark of pleasure he was kindling within her, but before it reached its pinnacle she heard Logan's thick gasp as he abruptly stiffened and then shuddered in release.

113

She lay still as he rolled away from her with a self-recriminatory curse. "I'm sorry," he muttered thickly.

Marnie tentatively reached out to touch his shoulder. "Logan, it's all right."

"No, it isn't. Damn!" He rested his forearm across his eyes. "I do nothing but dream about making love to you for the past three months and when my dream becomes a reality I blow it."

"Was it something I did?" she asked with an uncertainty that was unusual for her. But where her own sexuality was concerned, Marnie was not all that self-assured. Her own experience was limited to a three-year relationship with a man she'd met in her first year of college. Sex with Jeff had been pleasant but never the all-consuming ecstasy she'd read about. But then she doubted her ability to handle relinquishing control that completely.

"It was nothing you did," Logan quietly assured her. "It was my fault."

Marnie replied just as quietly, "I didn't ask in an effort to assign blame, Logan. These things happen."

"If I hadn't been so damn eager tonight . . ."

"I wasn't exactly a shrinking violet myself," she reminded him with a smile.

"No." Lifting his shielding arm from his face, he sent her a look both rueful and loving. "You're a warm, passionate woman who's got every right to be furious with me."

"I'm not furious. Just tired." She blinked owlishly, but the effort to keep her eyes open was too great for her. "Do you mind if I rest for just a minute?" Her murmured question was muffled by the pillow she'd already nuzzled into.

Logan turned onto his side and watched her sleeping face. "Go to sleep, Scarlett," he whispered. "Tomorrow's another day."

Marnie slept deeply. It was early morning when her slumbers were suspended by the feel of a cajoling finger circling the peak of her breast. The teasing caress blended into her dreams as she hovered on the threshold of wakefulness. In her dream the bewitching finger was replaced by a warm, molding palm, which was in turn supplanted by a moist, nuzzling mouth. She was then treated to a lavish display by a cajoling tongue that swirled seductively, and nibbling teeth that tugged erotically. A low moan of sleepy pleasure escaped her throat as a shimmering waterfall of sensations nudged her awake.

Their lashes fluttering in bemusement, her eyes opened. It was Logan's face that they saw, and having identified the source of her pleasure, they drifted shut again. But when his hand slid lower to seduce the most sensitive part of her body, she jerked awake.

"Don't pull away from me," he murmured, dropping feather-light kisses onto her mouth.

Marnie's defenses were still down from her slumbers, and she responded to his intensely evocative caresses with an abandon she found altogether frightening. Her scrambled mind hurriedly attempted to regain control, determinedly holding back the fluctuating tides of passion.

With the sensitivity of a lover, Logan immediately sensed her reticence to let go. The tempo of his caresses switched from erotic temptation to soothing tenderness. "What are you afraid of?"

Her reply was voiced in a half sob: "Losing control."

Cupping her cheek with one hand, he turned her face to his. His gaze was tenderly direct. "Last night I completely lost control with you. But, honey, that phrase is inaccurate. You don't lose anything by letting yourself go, you gain something very special." His voice lured her with its velvety

115

tone. "Let me show you." His thumb hypnotically grazed the tip of her breast.

There was no need to dominate evident in his touch, only a wish to share the sharply exquisite ecstasy she'd given him the night before. Beneath his gentle bidding, Marnie's limbs relaxed and unfolded like a tightly closed bud opening to the sun.

His hand trailed over her stomach, branching out over the curve of her hipbone before sliding home to the junction of her thighs. There he tantalized her with feathery tracings that hovered near but never entered the realm of her femininity. He soon expanded his sensual survey to include the delicate, ultrasensitive places unknown even to her. An aching need welled up from deep within her, a flutter transformed into a fine shaft of intense longing. Her legs shifted restlessly, and her hips rose in silent assent.

Logan partially granted her wish, his fingers becoming bolder and devoting themselves to the area that begged for attention. Marnie's breath caught in her throat at the wealth of sensations flowing through her. While his finger play satisfied her on one level, it also served to thrust her onto the next plane—a breathless, throbbing plateau she'd never visited before.

Logan's words of encouragement fueled her trip, as he watched the hunger take shape on her face. Her lips were parted, her eyes closed, her cheeks flushed with desire for him. Her body was warm and willing beneath his, so warm and willing that for a moment Logan felt his own desire threaten to overwhelm him.

But he held firm against his own needs and continued to incite hers. His dedicated pursuit of her pleasure was rewarded as Marnie shivered with ecstasy. Only then did he fuse his flesh to hers with a silky smoothness made all the more satisfying by its heady combination of gliding dalliance and impelling motion.

Her eyes flicked open in mute shock at the unadulterated joy he created within her. Her mouth rounded in sensual surprise at the increased satisfaction provided by each slow, heated stroke of his hard body. Her sighs became raspy feminine moans with the ever-tightening coil of building anticipation.

"Logan . . ." She gasped, frightened by the prodigious power being generated by their union.

"Don't hold back," he said urgently. "Feel it, move with it . . ."

She did, and her conscious mind was flooded with so much pleasure that it temporarily shut down. Thought was replaced by sensations—and incredible sensations they were! Linked to every fluctuating nuance of Logan's skillful thrusts, they began as a tensing ripple that grew into powerful propulsions.

"Lo . . . gan!" She panted, her nails digging into his back. "Oh . . . my . . . God."

"That's it, Scarlett," he crooned, never letting up for a moment. His increased rhythm matched her internal contractions so precisely that Marnie's entire being silently screamed and then shuddered in release.

Feeling the moment he'd been waiting for, Logan shouted his own release and followed her over the edge.

Marnie's thought processes came back with an almost drugged slowness. By then Logan lay beside her, and her head rested on his damp shoulder. Her pleasure-soaked body still felt deliciously pliant.

"Well? Does it feel like you lost something, Marnie?" His fingers smoothed her hair.

She nodded and answered in a languid voice. "My mind—

my heart." Her hand moved to rest over his heart. "I love you."

He tensed beside her. "You're just saying that because I've shown you paradise." His throbbing heart gave away the real feeling behind his joking remark.

She shook her head without bothering to lift it from his shoulder. "I'm saying it because it's true. I love you." She kissed the hollow of his shoulder, her tongue drinking in his salty taste. "I loved you before you showed me paradise."

"How long before?"

"You want the exact moment it happened?"

"Yes."

"I realized it while we were at Myrtle Beach," she obligingly told him, "but it had been creeping up on me for some time before that."

"Aren't you going to ask me if I love you?"

Again she shook her head. "When you're ready you'll tell me how you feel."

"As I once told you in your office, I've been ready since I first met you. I love you, Scarlett." He turned her face up to his. "Sometimes it feels like I always have."

Their lips met in a kiss unlike any other, for this one contained a new element: commitment. Commitment as yet unspoken, but powerful nonetheless.

CHAPTER SEVEN

Their lovemaking, glorious though it was, didn't change the fast-paced world in which they lived and worked. As the autumn progressed, Logan and Marnie often found themselves kept apart by their busy work schedules. Although they spent what time they could together, both longed for more than the snatched hours they were currently limited to.

Determined to do something about the situation, Marnie had come up with a temporary solution.

"What've you got there?" Diane asked Marnie, who came back from lunch one blustery November day with a handful of brochures.

"I stopped at my travel agent."

"Oh? Are you planning a trip?"

Marnie grinned like a Cheshire cat. "Could be."

By the end of the afternoon Marnie had gotten Tom's approval to use some of her vacation days to extend the upcoming Thanksgiving holiday. Then she checked availability with her travel agent and prepared to launch her campaign.

Tonight was one of the few nights both Marnie and Logan had free, and they were celebrating the rare occasion by sharing an intimate dinner for two at his place. Marnie had let herself in with the key he'd given her and had immediately set to work preparing her specialty, pecan pie. By the time Logan's car pulled up out front, she'd already blended the chopped pecans, corn syrup, brown sugar, eggs, and spices that comprised the traditional southern dessert, and was pouring the mixture into a pie shell.

She carefully popped the pie into the oven and went to greet Logan with a kiss.

"Mmmm, that's the kind of welcome I like," he murmured against her lips.

As was their custom, Marnie and Logan both worked on the dinner preparations. Tonight Marnie insisted on setting the table and left Logan to peel carrots in the kitchen while she stepped into the dining room and artfully arranged the travel brochures on the table's butcher-block surface. She tilted her head and studied the overall effect. Something was missing. Aha!

Whirling away, Marnie quickly dashed into his bedroom and triumphantly snatched up the Hawaiian hula dancer she'd won for him at the Myrtle Beach amusement park. Sure enough, the gyrating doll made a perfect centerpiece!

Now that the stage was set, she called in her audience. "Logan, I need your help a second."

"I'll be right there." He pushed through the kitchen's swinging café doors and viewed the cluttered table in amused surprise. "What's all this?"

"I'm thinking of taking a vacation," she announced.

"Alone?" he asked immediately.

Her lips lifted in a seductive smile. "It's not much fun taking a vacation alone."

Logan looked up from the brochure he'd been thumbing through to murmur, "You've got that right."

When he looked at her in that special way, Marnie had a hard time remembering what she was going to say. The longer she knew him, the more he affected her, because now she knew exactly where those special looks could take her! To paradise. Unfortunately the rest of the world intruded far too soon into their paradise. Which is why she'd gone to her travel agent to book them into the Paradise Beach Resort.

"How do you feel about Thanksgiving in the Caribbean?"

Despite the carefully laid-out props, her question caught him off guard. "Are you serious?"

Marnie ran a seductive hand down his arm. "Can't you tell?"

"You are serious!"

"Why are you so surprised?" She couldn't help feeling somewhat peeved by his reaction.

"Because it sounds to me, Dr. Lathrope, as if you're inviting me down to some tropical island for the express purpose of an intimate rendezvous." He eyed her with tender humor.

Marnie pretended to contemplate his words a moment before happily agreeing: "You're absolutely correct. I want to wake up next to you in the morning and not have to worry about your filming schedule, or my patient load, or anything else for that matter. I think we need this time away together."

Logan tugged her into his arms and nuzzled his lips against her luxuriant hair. "I think so too."

"Will you be able to get away?" She directed her question into the warm cotton of his shirt.

He promised, "I'll manage it somehow," and sure enough, he did.

Thanksgiving was cloudy and drizzly when Logan and Marnie's plane took off from Charleston's small airport. It was hot and muggy when they landed in Miami's huge terminal for their connecting flight to Saint Martin in the French West Indies or the Netherlands Antilles, depending on your perspective. Actually, the island had long ago been divided into two halves—one Dutch, the other French. Relations between the two were amicable, and tourists could easily travel from one side to the other.

As their travel itinerary promised, their next flight went directly to Saint Martin . . . but only after making scheduled stops in Puerto Rico and Antigua first.

"I think I'm going to fire my travel agent," Marnie said in a faint voice after their fourth takeoff of the day. The short runways of the islands' airports called for a very steep ascent, something her stomach did not appreciate.

Marnie had never been susceptible to airsickness before, but then she'd never flown before with a pilot who thought he was Buck Rogers! Even Air Force flights hadn't been this bad, and that was saying something.

By the time they deplaned on Saint Martin, it was ten at night local time. Once they'd passed customs and collected their baggage, a courtesy shuttle bus was waiting to transport them from the airport to their resort. Marnie's fingers clung to the back of the seat in front of her as their driver whisked them up roads that felt like they were on a forty-five-degree angle—*felt* being the operative word, since she couldn't see more than ten feet in front of the van. Logan, meanwhile, was kept busy wrapping one protective arm around Marnie and another around their luggage to prevent it from avalanching on top of them.

There was more excitement awaiting them when they arrived at the resort's front desk to check in. A beautiful woman with the dusky skin of the islands greeted them with a smile. "Welcome to Paradise Beach Resort."

Marnie was grateful that the usual "How was your flight?" hadn't been tacked on. That gratitude turned to concern, however, when Logan gave their names and the woman frowned over her reservations sheet.

"McCallister and Lathrope," she repeated.

"That's right," he confirmed. "Or it could be under Lathrope and McCallister."

"I'm sorry, sir. There seems to be some problem. Do you

have your reservation confirmation voucher?"

Marnie finally found it, at the very bottom of her carry-on shoulder bag.

"What's the problem?" Logan demanded while Marnie stuffed her assorted belongings back into her bag.

The desk clerk compared their confirmation voucher with a computer printout that lay on a desk in one corner. The news she broke to them was not good. "I'm afraid your reservations show up on the computer as being canceled."

"Obviously your computer has made an error," Logan retorted.

"Not to worry, sir." She smiled, waving her hand nonchalantly. "Everything will work out. We do happen to have a room available." She reached under the counter and pulled out a key. "The driver will take you up to your villa."

By this time Marnie was too exhausted to care where the room was, so long as it had a bed in it. She was dead tired. Thankfully their second van ride was short. After passing a lantern-lit building that appeared to be a restaurant, they headed up another hill.

"Here we are," their driver informed them a few moments later. He grabbed their two cases and led them up three flights of stairs. The last set of steps was the kicker, for they were spiral and very narrow.

"We've been banished to the tower," Logan murmured with rueful humor.

In the space of time it took Logan to tip their chauffeur/bellboy, Marnie had kicked off her shoes and visited the bathroom to rinse off her makeup. By the time Logan had closed the door behind the departing resort employee, Marnie was heading straight for the bed whereupon she lay down with a sigh and promptly fell asleep.

Logan gazed tenderly at her fully clothed figure. "Poor

baby," he whispered, stroking a strand of her colorful hair away from her mouth. "Poor me," he added as he undressed her and tucked her in, much as a father would do for a sleeping child. This was not the way he'd anticipated spending their first night in paradise!

Marnie woke the next morning feeling well rested and ready to love her man. The object of her sexy intentions was still asleep, his arm curved around her shoulder, his face relaxed in repose. Yielding gratefully to the urge, she proceeded to study Logan with avid, loving eyes. He had kicked the sheet down to his hips, where it lay in a tangled swath that was as provocatively placed as any fig leaf.

Her gaze roved over him for an evocative once-over before returning to his face and starting again, this time in a slower scrutiny. She looked at him as if for the first time, marveling at the angular structure of his face, the sensual fullness of his lips, the thickness of his lashes. Her eyes traced a triangular course from his collarbone to his strong shoulders and back up again.

Unable to resist temptation any longer, Marnie reached out to stroke what she'd seen, her fingertips adoring the satin-sheathed muscles of his chest. Her skin appeared pale compared with the tawny darkness of his. One of the many things she'd discovered about Logan was that he tanned easily and retained his tan long after summer had gone.

Her visual voyage continued as her eyes skimmed downward, over the flatness of his abdomen, the inward hollow of his navel, to the ridge of his hipbone. She lingered over the only part of him that was covered, her heart pounding as she remembered how incredibly good he felt. Reluctantly her eyes moved on to take in the powerful length of his thighs, the rounded bend of his knees, the powerful muscles of his calves, and his surprisingly well-shaped feet.

The sound of his voice drew her attention all the way up to the kissable curve of his mouth. "G'mornin'," he drawled, blinking somewhat sleepily.

"G'mornin'," she repeated. "I've got something for you."

His eyes darkened at the sirenlike seductiveness of her manner. "Is that so?"

"Mmm." She wet her lips with a tongue that was distinctly enticing. "Are you going to come get it?"

Opening his arms, he said in a husky voice, "I'd rather you came here and gave it to me."

"It would be my pleasure," she purred, shifting into a position that he found to be excruciatingly pleasurable.

Like a Botticelli angel, Marnie hovered over him, her mouth celebrating the special taste of his skin, her fingers massaging the rippling landscape of his body. Logan thrust his fingers through her fiery hair, guiding her tempting tongue up to his parted lips. Their kiss was dark and sweet, involving tongue touches that were intensely evocative of the merging yet to come.

Desire danced within her at the feel of his increased arousal, prompting her to act swiftly and with instinctive expertise. Her body was sultry and slick as she wrapped herself around him, drawing him into her welcoming warmth.

Logan surged upward, striving to reach the molten core of her inner fire, and with each lifting thrust he heightened her pleasure. Marnie fell into his rhythm, an undulant motion that took deep possession of her pliant body. Her trembling fingers kneaded his shoulders in exquisite satisfaction as untapped muscles were brought into play, registering and relaying sharply increasing waves of ecstasy.

The penetrating tremors swiftly spread, producing an erotic explosion that left Marnie melting in his arms. In contrast Logan's entire body stiffened as he reached his own peak and groaned in supreme satisfaction.

She treasured their continued closeness as Logan carried her with him in a smooth roll that brought them to their sides. Now they lay nose to nose, Logan's hands softly trailing over skin whose nerve endings still hummed.

He took advantage of Marnie's excessive sensitivity by blowing on her softly—from her temple to her breast. His mouth was close enough for a kiss, but the erotic stream of air caused more havoc than any kiss as he deliberately directed the flow of air over the darkened aureole of her breast. The peak tautened immediately.

Surprised by the instant response he'd elicited, she imitated his actions, curious to see if his response would be as intense. She began by blowing in his ear and was delighted to feel a tremor ripple through him. Intimately connected as they still were, she was able to experience his most minute reaction as if it were her own.

Marnie's eyes, gleaming with passionate discovery, met Logan's eyes, which were darkening with renewed desire. She lay watching his lids half close as she teasingly blew a dark curl away from his forehead. She then aimed her airborne caress over his lips, the underside of his chin, and the tip of his shoulder.

On and on, her investigations progressed, and all the while his lower torso was becoming increasingly firm until she exclaimed, "Logan! You're ready . . ."

Impelling her onto her back, he completed her half-gasped sentence. "To take you to paradise. . . ."

And so he did, with mind-shattering speed.

The next time Marnie opened her eyes, the sun filtering through the curtains had intensified. Dreamily wondering what time it was, she absently stroked the bare masculine chest she was resting upon.

Logan drowsily lifted one eyelid and teasingly moaned, "No more, Scarlett! You've worn me out."

"Logan, honey," she drawled. "If you can't tell the difference between a loving touch"—she repeated the stroke to his chest—"and one that means business"—her hand lowered to boldly stroke a much more intimate part of his anatomy—"then we're in trouble!"

"I'd say we're in trouble either way." He groaned, coming to life beneath her sexy ministrations.

"Funny, you don't feel worn out," she impishly stated.

"No? Neither do you," he noted, his own fingers seeking out her feminine center. "You feel like hot honey, all warm and inviting." His compliments and evocative explorations became increasingly intimate, until she gasped aloud and drew him to her.

This time their lovemaking was slow and infinitely pleasurable, leaving them both breathless and happy afterward.

It was some time before Marnie could speak. "You wicked man, you!" Even now her voice was still a mere throaty whisper.

"And don't you forget it." His whisper was equally raspy.

"Never." She kissed his shoulder.

"Now, let me see, that was a loving touch, right?" He waited until she'd nodded before roguishly adding, "Now I see the difference!"

"I should hope so, after a dramatic demonstration like the one we just shared."

"How about sharing some breakfast," Logan said. "I'm starved."

"Now that you mention it, so am I. What time do you think it is?"

Logan consulted his quartz watch, which lay on the rattan bedside table. "One in the afternoon."

Instantly Marnie was sitting bolt upright, her face a perfect picture of flushed astonishment. "You're kidding!"

"I assure you I'm not."

She jumped out of bed and grabbed a silk robe that lay atop her still-packed suitcase. Seeing he was still in bed, admiring her, she said, "Logan, you've got to get up."

"Again?" He teased her with earthy humor.

Marnie tossed her pillow at him before scampering away to pull back the tropical-print drapes. The view spread out before her was well worth the three-flight climb up to their tower room. The entire resort was built in the embracing arms of verdant rolling hills and faced the ocean. The water, a swirling tapestry of color ranging from teal to turquoise, smoothly lapped onto a horseshoe-shaped beach. Along the right edge jagged rock formations frothed up the otherwise peaceful surf. And off in the distance were the blue-smudged landmasses of neighboring islands, probably Saint Barts and Saint Kitts.

"Logan, come look at this." She called his name excitedly. When he joined her a second later, as naked as the day he was born, her excitement had turned to mild shock: "Logan! What if someone should look in?"

He shot her a naughty grin. "They'd have to be a sea gull to see anything interesting."

He was right; the windowsill hit him at midnavel, thus preserving his modesty.

"Even so, I think we should get dressed."

Logan sighed with mocking regret. "If you insist."

She teased him in return: "We can always buy you a grass skirt."

"Grass skirts are from the Pacific Islands, not the Caribbean," he informed her while tugging some clothes from his soft-sided suitcase.

It's true, they didn't come across any grass skirts on their first shopping trip in the Dutch capital of Philipsburg, but they did find a complete selection of South Seas sarongs. Seeing the way Logan appreciatively eyed the lissome store owner's colorful batik wrap, Marnie decided to buy a few for herself. They came in a straw carrying case complete with wrapping instructions.

"Where are the *un*wrapping instructions?" Logan roguishly questioned Marnie as they left the store.

"I'm sure you'll be able to figure them out by yourself," she stated with teasing demureness.

They wandered in and out of countless shops before stopping for an early dinner at a Front Street restaurant. Named after a famous town on the Italian Riviera, the restaurant had its own beautiful coastal view. Colorful umbrellas shaded patio-side tables. The cooling sea breeze carried the promising aromas wafting from the kitchen. Verdant hills and a sandy beach formed the semicircle of Great Bay, where numerous boats bobbed in the gentle waters.

"This is the life!" Marnie exclaimed when the fresh lobster tails she'd ordered were placed before her a short while later. Each was as big as her hand, and the dish was garnished with paprika, parsley, and fresh lemon. A bowl of drawn butter was placed nearby, as was a basket of freshly baked dinner rolls brushed with Parmesan cheese.

Logan's red snapper and side order of homemade pasta looked equally mouthwatering.

The meal was only one of many they enjoyed during their week-long stay in Saint Martin. They danced to the beat of steel bands and frolicked in the tepid Caribbean. They enjoyed a romantic sunset cruise and hiked over lush green hills. Several days were spent exploring the French side of the bipartite island and shopping in the French capital of Marigot.

Here the atmosphere was more tropical in flavor. An open market featuring foods and crafts from neighboring islands added to the exotic ambience. Yet Marigot's stores carried the finest French perfumes and European designers' clothing.

Their last afternoon on the island Marnie modeled her new purchases. Logan was already waiting for her out on their cantilevered back deck when she strolled out seductively. Her original hand-dyed batik resort wear was an artistic creation in turquoise and white, but Logan was not paying attention to the lavish floral design. Instead he observed with apparent appreciation the snug fit of the halter top and the ingenious simplicity of its design. The wraparound skirt rode provocatively low on her hips, depending on the natural curves of her body for a great deal of its support!

Marnie was too caught up in her own appraisal of Logan to be aware of his equally provocative evaluation of her. The reason for her openmouthed wonder was the racy black swimsuit she'd bought for him as a lark in Marigot. Not only did the suit's minuscule size leave ninety-nine percent of him bare, the way the slinky material clung to his masculine shape was downright indecent! Marnie's blood pressure immediately shot up!

Finally, in a husky voice, Logan said, "Very sexy, Scarlett."

"I could say the same about you," she said breathily.

"This suit is smaller than a postage stamp," he declared ruefully.

"Nonsense. I've seen suits smaller."

"Oh? Where?"

"Right here." A flick of her fingers undid her batik top and drew it away to reveal the daring line of the French string bikini she'd picked up for herself in Marigot.

"What do you think?" she questioned, her rapid breathing nearly dislodging the triangular bits of turquoise silk that were attempting to cover her breasts.

"You know I'm a man of action rather than words, Scarlett. Why don't I just show you what I think?"

Marnie wasn't even able to unwrap her batik skirt before Logan had wrapped her in his arms and scooted her over to the picnic table intended for outdoor meals. Once there, Logan perched on the tabletop and tugged her into the open V of his legs. His bare knees pressed against her hips in an erotic entrapment.

His mouth was at the exact height of her bikini top and he made good use of the advantageous position. His lips homed in on the bare skin between her breasts. From there he began ever-widening forays toward the curving slopes of her creamy skin. Logan was fascinated by her freckles, and he made a point of swirling the wet tip of his tongue over each one he found. As a redhead, Marnie had more than her fair share of freckles, and for once she was grateful for that!

Closing her eyes, she arched backward, thereby projecting her eager breasts forward. Her trembling fingers embedded themselves in the silky darkness of his hair as she held him to her. Wrapped in a web of sensual excitement, Marnie writhed against his open mouth and was rewarded with a ravishing nip from his white teeth.

"That should give you the general idea," he murmured against her bare skin. "For a more detailed description you'd have to step into my parlor."

Logan took a pleasure-dazed Marnie by the hand and hustled her over to the door. While waiting for him to open it, she placed a string of tiny kisses across his bare shoulder, her hand stealing around his waist.

"Marnie . . ." His hand stopped hers before it could skim over his taut virility.

"Hmmm?"

"Did you close the door on your way out here?"

"Probably." She dreamily placed another kiss on his shoulder before asking, "Why?"

"Nothing important. It's just that you've managed to lock us out." He tugged on the unyielding knob to emphasize his statement.

"Not to worry." She spoke in the soothing manner common to the natives of the laid-back island. "We'll just unlock the door."

"Fine. Where's the key?"

"The key." She paused a moment. "Uhhh . . ."

"You did bring the key out with you, didn't you?"

"I didn't exactly have a pocket handy to stick it into," she said, as if to defend herself. "Where's your key?"

"In my pants pocket. Inside the room."

"Now what do we do?"

"This deck may be semiprivate, but it's not private enough for what I want to do with you." His eyes, now dark with desire, slid over her with expressive warmth. "Since that's the case, you'll just have to stay here while I go get help." Logan strode over to the balcony and tugged on it to test its strength.

"What are you doing?" she cried as he suddenly swung his leg over the railing.

"You can take that panicked look off your face. I'm not attempting to commit suicide in a fit of thwarted passion," he teasingly assured her.

"No?" She rushed over to stop him. "What would you call jumping from a third-story balcony?"

"I'm not going to jump, I'm going to lower myself carefully. There's a big difference." The steplike construction of

132

the hillside villas was such that the hill behind them was only about six feet beneath him.

Even so, Marnie saw danger ahead. "You can't go barefoot. Here . . ." She hurriedly tugged off her one-size-fits-all beach shoes and handed them to him.

Logan refused to take them, eyeing the footwear with distaste. "I'm not wearing those things."

"Would you rather land barefoot on a cactus?" she asked with the heavy patience of a parent speaking to a stubborn child.

"What cactus?"

"The one two inches from your left foot."

Logan looked down to confirm her observation. In light of the prickly thorns glistening in the sunlight, the shoes seemed the lesser of two evils. "All right, give me the damn shoes," he ordered. "If you laugh . . ." His voice trailed away warningly.

"I won't," she promised, although it was somewhat difficult to keep a straight face. Her shoes did look pretty ridiculous on his feet. Ridiculous was better than injured, however.

Marnie held her breath as he dropped to the ground, landing with the agility of a cat and barely missing the cactus. Flashing her a triumphant grin, Logan took off around the side of the building, in search of a resort employee who could let him back into their room.

"I'm telling you it was the most embarrassing moment of my life," Logan was saying later that night as they walked along a moonlit beach. The grains of sand were soft beneath their bare feet, like the tender crumbs of a fluffy pound cake. "When those two elderly women on the first floor answered my knock on their door, I thought they would faint. And then one of them—she was old enough to be my grandmother, mind you—gets this gleam in her eyes and asks me if I'm room service."

"It's amazing you got out of that room alive," Marnie observed with a muffled laugh.

"All I wanted to do was use the phone, but I doubt they believed me. Luckily, I caught sight of a maid who was doing up the rooms in the next unit, and she used her passkey to let me in."

"You poor man." Marnie commiserated with him, sliding her arm around his waist.

Compared with his attire earlier in the day, Logan's present choice of clothing was strictly proper. His crisp tan trousers even sported a mesh belt while his short-sleeved shirt conservatively had all but two of its buttons buttoned.

"If you're underdressed, these islands can be as dangerous as in the days when they were teeming with Carib Indians," he said with more than a touch of mocking humor.

"Carib Indians—aren't they the ones who smoked seven-inch cigars and ate people?"

Logan raised a brow at her description.

"I read that brochure from the tourist office, too, you know," she explained. "Amazing to think the Caribbean was named after a fierce tribe that's since disappeared."

"How'd you like the part about Pegleg Pete?"

"Refresh my memory."

"Peter Stuyvesant. You know, the one who was head of the Dutch West India Company, who said 'You can lead a horse to water, but you can't make him drink' and then went north to become the governor of New Amsterdam, more commonly known as New York."

"Oh, that Peter Stuyvesant," she murmured, nodding knowingly despite her confusion. "Where'd the Pegleg Pete come from?"

"He lost his leg in battle. History is unclear about whether it was his left or right leg, however, which made it tough for the statue makers who followed. Which to omit? Left or right?"

"Decision making can be difficult," Marnie agreed.

"I'm glad you made the decision for us to come down here." His dark voice reached out to caress her.

"To the beach?"

"To Saint Martin." He sat down on one of the webbed beach chairs provided by the resort, and tugged Marnie down beside him. "I'm glad we've had this time together."

"So am I." She leaned back against his chest, gazing out at the star-laden tropical sky and the glittering waves of the ocean.

They were on the Atlantic side of the island, the same Atlantic Ocean that edged Charleston and Myrtle Beach. Yet here it seemed more mellow. On the islands life was less harried, and there was plenty of time to enjoy its pleasures. But what would it be like when she and Logan returned to Charleston? Would they get caught up again in their jobs?

The feel of Logan's fingers at the base of her neck roused her from her troubling thoughts. A moment later she felt him slipping something over her head and fastening it around her bare throat.

"What's this?" she asked in surprise.

"A present."

Her curious fingers encountered a necklace of . . . "Seed pearls?"

Logan shook his head. "Garnets. I thought they were the most suitable choice—to go with your gorgeous hair, Scarlett."

Marnie kissed the compliment from Logan's lips, gratefully murmuring her words of thanks against his warm mouth. Surrendering to his embrace, she refused to acknowledge the tiny voice warning her that every paradise has its serpent.

CHAPTER EIGHT

The serpent in their paradise reared its ugly head less than a week after they had returned home to Charleston. Marnie had gotten tied up with a case at the Safe Place and was late arriving at Logan's beach house for the dinner they'd planned. It was the first time they'd eaten alone since Saint Martin. The few meals they had shared had been hurried affairs, since either Logan had had to get back to work or Marnie had had appointments scheduled.

She knew something was wrong the moment she stepped into the house. Although his dark green Datsun was parked outside, she saw no sign of Logan. "Anybody home?" she questioned the empty living room. There was no reply. Logan's favorite armchair was empty, as were the kitchen, bedroom, and single bathroom.

Marnie was beginning to worry when she caught sight of him through the sliding glass door that led out to the beach. He stood with his back to her, seemingly impervious to the chilly gale coming straight off the churning Atlantic. Having just come from outside, Marnie knew it was too cold to be out without a jacket of some kind. Grabbing up his favorite sweatshirt, she buttoned her own wool jacket and joined him.

Her concern grew when Logan offered no greeting and shook his head when she attempted to hand him his sweatshirt.

"Logan, it's cold out here." She almost had to shout to be heard over the pounding surf. "Please come inside."

He was still for so long that she wondered if he'd heard

137

her, and was about to repeat her plea when his shoulders lifted and dropped in a deep sigh and finally he turned to her. He reached for her with an almost blind desperation, holding her so tightly she could scarcely breathe.

Marnie welcomed his embrace and returned it with all her might, offering him her unspoken sympathy. He was hurting. She could feel the waves of anguish and frustration coming from him. What could have happened? His parents? His sisters? Had something terrible happened to them?

She repeated her request, this time directly into the ear her mouth was resting near. "Logan, come inside and talk to me."

Thankfully, this time he listened to her and nodded, partially releasing her as he turned them both toward the shelter of the house. Marnie directed him straight to his favorite armchair with its welcoming comfort and anxiously set him into it. Kneeling before him, she asked softly, "What is it? What's wrong?"

"Have you seen the news?"

She blinked in surprise. "The news? You mean the seven-o'clock news?"

He nodded.

"No, I haven't. Why? What's happened?"

Logan closed his eyes and wearily leaned his head back. "I was covering a story on a hostage situation. A man had barricaded himself into his house and was threatening to shoot his wife and himself."

Her softly spoken "Oh, Logan . . ." came out unbidden. She had a horrifying idea she knew what was coming next.

"The police records indicate that this man had threatened his wife before and the authorities hadn't taken the situation seriously." He opened his eyes to look at her, shadows darkening their sherry depths. "But you would have taken his threats seriously, wouldn't you, Marnie? You would have tried to help his wife, wouldn't you?"

She nodded slowly.

"That's right." His voice was harsh with emotion, his face drawn with pain. "You would have tried to save his wife and probably gotten yourself shot and killed in the process. He did kill her, you know. We heard the shot from where we were waiting outside, but there was nothing the police could do. He was still armed, he might have shot someone else. The guy finally surrendered about an hour later. Came out with his hands up, and in front of the television cameras he directed his small pistol to his head and killed himself. Right there on film. It was the leading story on tonight's broadcast."

"Oh, Logan, I'm so sorry."

"No lectures about televised violence?"

She shook her head and reached out to trace with soothing fingers the taut line of his jaw. She could read in his eyes the regret he felt at having the tragedy sensationalized. "I just want to hold you and ease you through the pain."

"You don't understand." He gripped her arms. "It could have been you."

Marnie looked at him in bewilderment. "What could have been me?"

"It could have been you who was killed!" His haunted gaze matched the raw intensity of his voice. "You deal with these women all the time, and that means you deal with their husbands, husbands who are capable of extreme physical violence—even murder."

"Logan, I don't deal with the husbands," she explained patiently. "That's why the shelter's location is kept secret, so the husbands can't find their wives and endanger their safety."

"How long do you think you can keep the location a secret?" he demanded.

"We've managed pretty well so far."

"Have you?" The tone of his voice had become disturbingly cynical.

"Yes."

"*I* know where the shelter is."

His curt words left Marnie stunned. "What?"

"I know where the shelter is," he bleakly repeated. "I've known all along. I followed you right to it."

The shock of betrayal swept over her in an overwhelming rush, chilling her skin and stifling her breath. "Logan, how could you?"

He deliberately mistook her question. "It was easy. Anyone could have done it. That's what I'm afraid of."

"I can't believe I'm hearing you correctly," Marnie exclaimed in a shaken voice.

"I did it for you."

She pulled away and stared at him with accusing brown eyes. "I trusted you!"

"You didn't trust me enough to tell me where the shelter was," he shot back.

"It's not a matter of trust. It would have been a serious breach of professional ethics for me to tell you the address of the shelter. I thought you understood that. I thought that's why you didn't question me about it. But that was all a sham, wasn't it?" Her voice was bitter. "You knew all along."

Logan stood and raked an impatient hand through his wind-tousled hair. "Marnie, you don't understand what I'm getting at here. If I followed you, then so could one of the men looking for that shelter. Thanks to my special reports about wife abuse, they know you work at the medical center. All they'd have to do is follow you from there to the Safe Place."

"I never go directly to the Safe Place from my office," she pointed out coldly.

"So you go home for a few hours first, whatever." The slashing gesture of his hand erased her statement. "My point is, you could still be followed, and that's too dangerous." His voice deepened with emotion. "I love you. I don't want anything happening to you."

Her anger remained undiminished. "Logan, you've interfered in the business of my profession. As a psychologist, I can't have my lover following me when I go to see patients."

"How about your husband?" he grated.

"Husband?"

"I want to marry you. I don't want you working at the shelter anymore. It's too dangerous." Alarmed by her sudden silence, he spoke now in anger: "If you really love me, you will do as I ask."

To which Marnie retorted, "If you really loved me, you wouldn't ask me to do this."

"I do love you, and I am asking you." He paused to take a deep breath. "Please quit your counseling at the shelter." His voice was calmer now as he offered a compromise: "At least until they get some sort of security system installed."

"Logan, that could be years. Those women need me now. I can't let them down."

"What about me?" His voice turned grim. "I need you too. Would you rather let me down?"

"Of course not!" she answered in exasperation.

"Then what's it going to be?" he asked starkly. "The shelter or me?"

"I can't answer that question."

Logan's face froze. "You just did." He turned abruptly and headed for the front door.

"Where are you going?" she cried out in alarm.

"Out."

"Logan, wait! Logan! We have to talk about this."

"There's nothing left to say." His toneless words held an unmistakable finality.

Marnie stared at the closed door with blank eyes. He'd left. He'd dropped a bombshell on her and then left. Walked out because she wouldn't choose him over her work.

The entire incident, coming as it did with the brutal suddenness of the unforeseen, left her shell-shocked. Logan had asked her to marry him. But he'd made demands on her that she couldn't meet. She wiped the tears that welled from her eyes.

This was no time to cry. She had to notify Gwen about the breach in the Safe Place's security. Logan knew the address, but she had yet to discover if he'd told anyone else. Chances were he hadn't, but, then, at one time she would have said chances were he would never follow her in the first place.

To think she'd interpreted his silence on the subject as a show of his faith in her capabilities. Some kind of faith! What he'd done went against everything she believed in, and blinded her to his reasons and motivations. The hurt she was experiencing went too deep to allow objective thinking.

"I guess dinner's off," she heard herself mumbling, and laughed almost hysterically at the utter inanity of her comment. "Yes, dinner's off, the whole thing's off!" She choked back a sob.

"I am not going to fall apart," she maintained, biting her trembling lower lip with fierce determination.

Marnie made the twenty-five-minute drive back to her home, and once there, she had no clear recollection of how she had even gotten there. The moment she got inside she phoned Gwen Davis and briefly told her what had happened. Although Gwen had been understanding, Marnie couldn't help feeling responsible.

In an effort to assuage that guilt Marnie spent even more

time at the shelter during the next few days. There was always work to be done, and the activity helped keep her mind off Logan. At least that was her intention, but it never really worked. Logan was never far from her thoughts.

The nights were the worst, when she lay in bed in the lonely predawn hours, hugging the oversize panda bear Logan had won for her that fateful Saturday in Myrtle Beach. *Panda-monium,* he'd named it, and that was exactly what he'd brought into her life. She switched on her bedside lamp and then resolutely carried the panda to her closet and stuffed it inside.

But the thought of the fuzzy toy animal being locked in the darkness proved to be too hard to bear. Laughing bitterly at her unintentional pun, Marnie relented and left the door open. Crawling back into bed, she switched off the light and curled into a tight little ball, feeling cold and incredibly alone.

At the office, Diane and Elaine both knew something was terribly wrong when Marnie's brown eyes reflected dull remoteness instead of their customary zest for life.

Diane, in her usual forthright way, was the first to confront Marnie.

"You look like you've lost your best friend. Is there something I can do to help?"

"No, Diane. Thank you for the offer." Her voice lacked any real emotion.

"It's something to do with Logan, isn't it?" Diane astutely guessed.

"We've got more important things to do than sit around discussing personal problems," Marnie stated with aloof disapproval. "Do you have the Jenkins file?"

"It's already on your desk."

Marnie found the file and immediately opened it, pretending a deep immersion in its contents.

Diane was not fooled. "When I broke up with George last year, you helped me through it. I'm just offering to repay the favor," she quietly told Marnie before leaving.

Rand was the next in line to offer a sympathetic shoulder. "I don't know what went wrong between you two, and I won't butt into your business by asking. But I do have one thing to tell you. And that is that I've never seen a guy as much in love as Logan was with you. I mean, Marnie, the guy even gave up smoking for you."

"You don't understand." They were sitting in Rand's still-uncompleted living room. Drop cloths covered some of the furniture, and the smell of fresh plaster permeated the air. "He followed me to the shelter."

"He was worried about you."

"He destroyed my trust in him. And then he told me that I had to choose between him and my work. How can he say he loves me and then demand that I give up my work? I thought Logan was more enlightened than that, but at the first sign of trouble he reverted back to chauvinistic ideas."

"Logan's no chauvinist," Rand retorted. "He's simply a man in love who's worried about his woman's safety."

Marnie gave up trying to talk to Rand about it. He was obviously viewing the situation from a man's perspective and taking Logan's side. "I've got to go, Rand, I'll be late for work."

"Work?" Rand repeated. "At this time of night?"

But Marnie was already gone.

Elaine was also aware of Marnie's excessively demanding schedule and confronted her friend one day after work. "What would you say if one of your patients displayed such compulsive behavior?"

"I'm not compulsive," said Marnie, finishing the notes she was writing on a patient's file.

Elaine took the pen from Marnie's hand and closed the file Marnie had been working on. "Between the office and the shelter you're working ten- and twelve-hour days, seven days a week. I'd call that compulsive. Don't you think it's time you talked about what went wrong between you and Logan?"

Marnie ran a weary hand through her copper-colored hair. "I already told you what happened."

"Yes, you told me what happened. Logan followed you to find out where the shelter was located. I'm not talking about the facts, I'm talking about the emotions. How do you feel?"

"Hurt, betrayed." Marnie rose from her swivel chair and restlessly paced the office.

"How do you feel about Logan?"

Marnie paused in front of a Boston fern and fingered the lacy leaves. "I don't know how I feel. I can't seem to see past what he's done."

"A simple word of advice, Marnie. It's written on that poster you've got framed on your wall over there. The one that says 'Tragedy occurs when we'd rather be right than happy.' Don't let that happen to you, Marnie."

That night, for the first time since Logan had walked out on her nine days before, Marnie let the tears fall freely, soaking her pillowcase with their salty wetness. She still loved Logan, but her trust in him was badly shaken. How could love survive without trust?

Another sleepless night brought her no closer to an answer. Marnie was up and dressed before her alarm went off. It was Saturday, and another weekend without Logan. She had promised Gwen that she would fill in for her at the shelter today.

Marnie made herself a nutritious breakfast only to scrape it into the garbage. She drank three cups of coffee, black. She stared out her living-room window and blinked hard against the threatening prickle of another bout of crying.

"Love is hell," Marnie bitterly informed her tear-stained reflection on the rain-spattered glass.

"Love is hell," Logan bitterly informed his hollow-eyed reflection in the bathroom mirror. Tying one on with his buddies last night had only served to give him a splitting headache this morning—or was it afternoon?

He didn't know, and as was his wont these days, he didn't really care. Complete indifference, that was his rule from now on. No more involvements. No more of this self-maiming emotion called love.

Biting off a curse, Logan turned on the shower, deliberately selecting a mixture containing more cold water than hot. The action only served to remind him of all the cold showers he'd already taken because of Marnie. Shucking off his toweling robe, he stepped into the glass-enclosed shower stall.

"It's over." His declaration echoed around him.

Then why do you still love her?

"I'll get over her."

Do you really believe that? Her essence is in your bloodstream, her image in your heart.

Logan's heart thudded painfully as he recalled the glorious days and nights they'd shared in Saint Martin. She'd been the perfect lover and companion. She'd said she loved him. Yet when he'd asked her to marry him—something he'd never even thought to say to another woman—she'd chosen her work over him.

"Get that through your thick skull, McCallister!" His tone was harsh, his words a command. "It's over!"

Although it was a Saturday, Logan planned on going into work anyway. Some research material concerning his latest series on teenage alcoholism needed looking over. Anything to get him out of the beach house, where Marnie's memory confronted him at every turn. Searching through the bathroom cabinets for an aspirin for his pounding head, he came across a bottle of her cologne. Logan's jaw clenched in pain as he slammed the cabinet closed with a force that threatened the mirror.

Her silk robe still hung in his closet next to the blue shirt he grabbed. And in the kitchen, next to his jar of instant coffee, was the box of herbal tea she always drank. Muttering a curse, Logan stormed out of the house without eating breakfast. At least in the television studio he wouldn't be faced with constant reminders of Marnie.

The 280Z eagerly ate up the few miles between Sullivan's Island and Charleston. The rainy weather suited his mood; the cheerful Christmas music on the car radio did not. He switched to a bluegrass station, turned up to a high decibel level. By the time he arrived at the studio, his headache had grown to huge proportions.

Eliot Raleigh, veteran news director that he was, took one look at Logan's haggard face and hauled out the economy-size bottle of aspirin he kept in his bottom desk drawer.

"Here, you look like you could use a few of these."

Logan accepted the pills and swallowed them with a paper cupful of water from the water cooler. Crunching the cup between impatient fingers, he dropped it into the trash bin and sank into the chair facing Eliot's desk.

"Hey, no dame's worth it," the twice-divorced Eliot advised.

"Yeah, I know what you mean. Anything new on the news wires?"

"Naw, it's a slow day," Eliot reported. "Nothing goin' on; no disasters, no accidents, not even any major fires. It's the pits."

"You're all heart," Logan mocked.

"Ain't that the truth," Eliot drawled laconically. "You gonna work today or what?"

Logan shrugged and made a move to get up. "Might as well."

Eliot picked up his ringing phone and urgently motioned for Logan to remain seated. A few moments later he hung up the receiver with a distracted bang.

"Hot dog!" Eliot wiped an excited hand over his half-bald head. "We've hit pay dirt."

"Are you going to tell me or do I have to guess?"

"We've got another hostage situation. Do you believe our luck? Two in the past two weeks! I want you to go cover this one."

"Me? Why me?"

"Because you handled that last hostage deal so well and because you may be able to get an inside lead on this one."

Logan didn't like the sound of that. His stomach muscles tightened, their action a premonitory reflex. "What do you mean?"

Eliot confirmed Logan's worst fear. "You interviewed the woman being held. You remember—that shrink who works at the shelter for battered women."

"Marnie?" Logan's voice cracked.

But Eliot was too busy consulting his notes to notice the stricken expression on his reporter's face. "That's right. Dr. Marnie Lathrope." Eliot finally looked up to find Logan half out the door. "Hey, Logan, where are ya goin'? You don't even have the address yet. Damn it!" Eliot hollered, "Joe!"

The cameraman came racing into the news director's office.

"Get out there and follow Logan," Eliot ordered. "He's on

a hot story. Here's the address." He ripped a page off his notepad. "And get me some footage for tonight's show," he bellowed after Joe's fast-departing figure.

CHAPTER NINE

Saturday was always a particularly busy time at the Safe Place. It was noon before things temporarily quieted down. Marnie made good use of the momentary lull by working on the logbook, entering the new arrivals and departures. Her task was soon interrupted by one of the residents.

"What is it, Carolyn?" Marnie asked.

The woman made no reply, but her face was deathly pale.

Marnie got up and hurriedly walked around the desk. "Are you ill? Is there some kind of trouble?"

"You might say that, Dr. Lathrope," an unfamiliar male voice answered from the threshold, behind Carolyn. The intruder, a man in his early thirties, boldly stepped into the office.

Marnie tried to contain her shock at seeing a man in the shelter. "Who are you?"

"Doug Parker."

"Well, I'm sorry, Mr. Parker, but this shelter is off-limits to men."

"You don't even know who I am, do you?"

"It really doesn't matter who you are, Mr. Parker, you're still not allowed in here. I'm asking you to leave." Marnie's voice fairly crackled with authority.

The man reacted by whipping up a briefcase he held at his side. "You see this? You see these wires? This is a bomb, lady, and I've got enough explosives in here to blow this whole building to kingdom come, so I wouldn't be in such a hurry to get rid of me."

Marnie froze at the man's harsh words. Automatically her crisis-intervention training took over. *Stay calm. Use an even tone of voice.* "Why would you want to blow up the building?"

"Because you've ruined my life." Doug Parker came further into the small room that served as an office. Whirling to face the cringing Carolyn, he snarled, "And stop that whimpering. You sound just like my wife!"

"Come now, Mr. Parker. I'm sure you intend for Carolyn to be terrified. Isn't that what you're hoping to accomplish by coming here with a bomb?" Marnie's eyes slid to the man's wrist, where a handcuff linked him to the potentially deadly briefcase.

"I'm not interested in the other women here," Doug answered. "I want to terrify *you.*" He looked at Marnie with malicious intent.

Marnie bravely returned his gaze. "Why would you want to terrify me?"

"I told you. Because you've ruined my life!" Doug shouted in fury. "You broke up my marriage! I loved Pam, I loved my little boys, but you took them away from me. She's gone to Arizona, you know. She's filed for divorce. I got the papers today."

His wife's name was Pam. Pam Parker! The shelter's very first resident, the one who'd arrived on the Fourth of July before the Safe Place had even been officially opened. Pam had stayed at the shelter for two weeks waiting for money from her relatives in Arizona. Suddenly things fell into place.

Understanding the man's motivation helped Marnie sort out her options. "Since I'm the one you want to terrify, Mr. Parker, may all the other residents leave?"

Doug Parker wavered. "I don't know about that."

"There are children here, Mr. Parker. You wouldn't want

to hurt them, now, would you? Children like your own, Mr. Parker."

Doug wiped a nervous finger across his sweaty upper lip. "Okay, the kids can leave, but not the women."

"It's up to you, of course, Mr. Parker, but I would have thought that it would be easier to control just one woman, myself, than a houseful of them."

"Shut up," Doug snapped. "Shut up and let me think."

"May Carolyn take the children outside while you think, Mr. Parker?" Marnie asked with calm courtesy.

"All right," he said, reluctantly acceding to her request. "But remember, anyone else tries to get away and I'll blow the place up. I'd do it too," he added in case she didn't believe him.

"I know you would, Mr. Parker. No one else will leave right now. Go ahead, Carolyn. Tell the other women to stay in the main dining room, and then you go ahead and take the children outside."

Slowly Carolyn moved away from the wall.

"It will be all right, Carolyn," Marnie softly reassured her. "Go on now."

From his position near the office door Doug oversaw the children's departure. Once they'd gone, he muttered, "I love my kids, you know."

"I imagine you do, Mr. Parker. Thank you for letting them go."

It wasn't long after that that they heard the screech of approaching police sirens.

"I wondered when they'd get here," Doug said with disturbing calmness.

"Mr. Parker, this is Lieutenant Rierdon of the Charleston Police Department," a male voice announced over a bullhorn. "We'd like you to surrender and come on outside."

"Hey, you!" Doug pointed to one of the women gathered

in the dining room across the hall. "You go out there and tell them I'll blow the place up if anyone comes near me."

The woman hurriedly obeyed his command.

"Yeah, that's a good idea," Doug murmured. "I'll send each of those women outside with a message for the cops. I don't really need them in here anyway, not when I've got you." Again his interest focused on Marnie.

The ringing phone startled both of them, but Marnie hid her nervousness more successfully than Doug did.

"Answer it," he ordered.

Marnie did so. "Hello?"

"Dr. Lathrope?"

"Yes."

"This is Lieutenant Rierdon again. We're directly outside the building. We received the message. Are you all right? Have you or any of the women been hurt?"

"Who is it?" Doug demanded.

"It's the police."

Doug grabbed the phone from her with the growled warning "Don't make one move."

He then spoke into the phone. "Yeah, listen, I want the news media called in on this. I want my side of the story heard for a change. I want that guy who did the series on this shelter—McCallister. I want him to report the real story. Yeah, sure you can get back to me. But it had better be real soon," he added ominously before hanging up.

Marnie quickly gathered her thoughts. "If you're going to call the media in, then I guess you'll want to make a good impression so people will listen to you."

"Good impressions aren't worth bullshit in this world," Doug retorted bluntly. "People only listen to violence. You're only listening to me because I'm carrying this bomb here." He indicated the briefcase.

"Mr. Parker, had I known you wanted me to listen to you, I would have been glad to do so without your having to resort to violence," she assured him. "Since that's the case, won't you please reconsider and let the other women go?"

"I'll let them go when McCallister gets here." Doug again moved toward the door. "Hey, you with the long hair." He gestured toward another of the residents. "You go out and tell them I'll let you all go, except for the doc here, when that reporter gets here."

Nine residents remained in the shelter. Marnie was keeping track. Doug had released three, and three were out taking care of personal business.

The next time the phone rang, Doug answered it. "You got McCallister there? Good, let me talk to him."

Logan took the specially equipped police-car phone that was handed to him. His eyes were flinty with self-control; his face was pale and drawn. His tone of voice, however, was deliberately nonchalant. "This is McCallister."

"Listen, I'm going to give you an exclusive on this," Doug told him. "I want you to report on tonight's news that this shrink here is making a practice out of breaking up happy homes by filling women's heads with all that feminist bullshit."

"That may be true, Mr. . . . Parker—is that right?"

"The name's Doug Parker."

"Well, Doug, I don't mean to be blunt, but I'm not sure the public is going to be very receptive to you when you're holding women hostages. Now if you'll let the women go, then perhaps you and I can sit down and have a serious interview."

"I'm not crazy, McCallister. I know the cops are out there and that what I'm doing is illegal. But I was desperate, don't you see? No one was listening to me."

"Well, we're listening to you now, Doug."

"Only 'cause I'm holding these women."

"That may have been what grabbed our attention, but we'll keep listening to you even if you let the women go."

"Oh, yeah?" he asked skeptically.

"Listen, get the women out of there and I'll come in and talk to you."

"All right, I'll let the women go."

Logan closed his eyes in silent relief, his knuckles white from the unbearable tension as his hand gripped the receiver. *Thank God. Marnie will be safe.*

"I'll let the women go," Doug repeated. "All of them except for the shrink."

Logan's eyes shot open, and a frantic desperation flared in their depths. Although his throat felt clamped shut, he somehow managed to ask "Why keep the shrink?" in a neutral tone.

"Because she's the reason for all this," Doug told him. "She broke up my marriage. I'll let the other women go, I'm not unreasonable. But not the shrink. Take it or leave it."

The police officer, who'd been monitoring the call from another mobile extension, nodded to Logan and mouthed "Take it."

"Okay, let the other women go and I'll come in to talk to you," Logan said.

"Wait until the women come out and then you can come in. But only you, no one else," Doug warned. "And you'd better not be armed. I've got this briefcase set to go off whenever I want it to. Any trouble and I'll blow us all up."

"There won't be any trouble," Logan quietly assured him. "I'll come alone, unarmed."

Five minutes later all the shelter's residents were safely behind the police barricades, reunited with their frightened

155

children. Logan slowly approached the front door, holding his arms away from his body, palms open to show he was indeed unarmed.

Logan's heart was pounding so loud that he didn't even hear the hollow ring of his footsteps as he entered the building's tiled foyer. But Marnie heard the footsteps and silently murmured a prayer for Logan's safety. Although Doug had let the residents go free, she knew he was not making idle threats when he talked of blowing the building sky-high.

"Stay right there, McCallister," Doug ordered in a voice grown taut with nerves. "Take off the jacket."

Logan cautiously did so, making sure not to use any sudden moves that might trigger the already-strung-out man.

"Leave your jacket there and go sit on that chair. As you can see, I've got the explosives right here." Doug motioned to the expensive briefcase handcuffed to his left wrist. "So you just stay where you are and there shouldn't be any accidents."

"Where's Dr. Lathrope?" Logan asked with studied casualness.

"I locked her in the supply closet. You don't need to see her during this interview. It's me you came to talk to, right?" Doug's stance was belligerent and challenging.

Seeing the man's explosive reaction, Logan said hurriedly, "Of course I came to talk to you, Doug."

"Good, then listen to what I have to tell you."

Logan obligingly recorded, with Doug's permission, everything the man had to say. He asked all the right questions and kept Doug talking for as long as possible. But all the while Logan's real concern lay with Marnie. Repressing his protective instincts was extremely difficult when everything within him screamed to rescue the woman he loved. But he knew any rash rescue attempt would only serve to threaten Marnie's safety even further. So he sat there and listened.

"Now you go tell the people of Charleston what's really going on in here," Doug commanded. "Tell them I'm not crazy, that I love my wife very much, that everything that's happened here today is this shrink's fault."

Logan knew he had to play it cool. "What are you going to do with Dr. Lathrope?"

Doug shrugged, being careful not to jostle the briefcase. "I haven't decided yet. I'll let you know when I do."

"You know it would go easier for you if you let her go." Logan made the suggestion sound as if he were speaking in Doug's best interests. "You could hold me hostage instead."

"Why would I want to do that?"

"I'm better known than Dr. Lathrope is. You're bound to get more attention if I were the hostage."

"Probably. But I intend keeping Dr. Lathrope," Doug stated with implacable stubbornness. "Your time's up, McCallister. You can go now."

Leaving Marnie inside that house was the hardest thing Logan had ever been called upon to do in his life. But do it he did, for he had no choice. Walking down the front steps, he bowed his head and brokenly murmured, "Please, God, let her be all right."

While she was locked within the cramped, airless confines of the closet, Marnie had hung on to the sound of Logan's voice. He'd spoken with a sureness and a calm confidence that had given her strength. Closing her eyes, she could picture his face; his naughty grin, his loving eyes. The life-and-death consequences of their current situation wiped out all but the most fundamental of truths. She loved Logan. And she was determined to spend the rest of her life with him.

Doug was in a more positive frame of mind when he finally let Marnie out of the closet. But his temporary wave of triumphant elation soon swung to intense depression as the realization of what he'd done began to close in on him. The police still called every fifteen minutes, but Doug had stopped answering the phone himself. Instead he had had Marnie inform them that he wasn't ready to talk yet and then hang up.

Four hours after he'd taken her prisoner all the principals involved were reaching their breaking point.

Joe had accompanied Logan on many assignments, but never had he seen such utter torment reflected on the other man's face. Logan stood and stared at the shelter as if willing Doug Parker to release Marnie. He refused offers of warm cups of coffee and ignored the swarm of media people behind the barricades. His expression was bleak, but his eyes were blazing, glittering.

"She'll be all right," Joe felt compelled to reassure Logan. "She's a smart lady. She'll keep her cool. The police say the longer Parker talks, the smaller the chance is that he'll do anything rash."

"If he hurts her, I'll kill him," Logan vowed in a strained voice.

"I know, buddy, I know." Joe laid his hand on Logan's tensed arm. "Just take it easy. Things will work out."

"They've got to," Logan muttered, his eyes filled with mute despair. "They've just got to."

Meanwhile Doug's mood had sunk even lower. "There's no good way out of this mess now, is there?" Doug spoke with a blank despair Marnie knew she had to keep in check. A man with nothing to lose could be deadly.

"Doug, forget the police out there for a while." She tried to draw his attention away from the window—he had been staring at it for the past half hour. "You said you wanted to talk."

"I talked to McCallister."

"Did that make you feel better?"

Doug shrugged, the movement jiggling the metal of the handcuffs. "For a while it did. But it can't bring Pam and the kids back to me."

"I'm sorry things worked out as they did," Marnie said.

Doug turned to face Marnie accusingly. "Pam wouldn't have left if you hadn't pushed her."

"Pam left to stay alive," Marnie retorted bluntly. "But she also left so your children's love for you would stay alive. It's very painful for any child to see one parent abusing the other."

"I didn't mean to hurt Pam," Doug stated wearily. "She just made me mad sometimes."

"Anger can be a very destructive emotion. But it doesn't have to be. We can all learn to deal with anger, sometimes we just need help."

"I'm not crazy." Doug spat out the words.

"I never said you were." Marnie kept her voice on an even level. "I just said there are ways you can learn to deal with anger more effectively, just as there are ways you can learn to sell real estate more effectively or do your taxes more effectively." Marnie knew that she was simplifying things tremendously, but the analogy seemed to get through to Doug.

"You think I could get Pam back that way?"

Marnie sidestepped his question: "What do you think?"

"What would I have to do?"

Doug's question gave Marnie hope. "A friend of mine has set up a program for people who want to learn to control their anger."

"You mean a shrink?"

Marnie shook her head. "He's a counselor who works in a clinic. He deals with a lot of men and has helped them get rid of disruptive habits."

"You mean like those clinics where they get you to stop smoking?"

"I suppose you could say that." If such a concept was one Doug felt comfortable with, then that was fine. "It's a program dealing with rage and ways of handling it and avoiding it."

Marnie could see that Doug was seriously considering her words. There might be a way out of this after all.

Meanwhile Logan was having another consultation with the police. "I'm telling you, Parker's got the briefcase attached to him. There's no way you could wrestle it from him."

A member of the SWAT team said, "If we rushed the place, we might—"

"No way!" Logan grated. "He'd kill Marnie."

"Not if we got to him first."

"And if you don't?" Logan shot back.

"McCallister's right," Lieutenant Rierdon maintained. "The hostage's safety has to be our first priority. We'll wait."

Logan took a deep breath and said, "Thank you, Lieutenant."

"Hey, McCallister, give us a break," one of his compatriots demanded as Logan passed within calling distance. "Tell us what's going on."

"What exactly is your relationship with the hostage?" another reporter asked.

"Is it true that you and Dr. Lathrope were romantically involved at one time?" a third person probed.

Logan ignored them all as he resumed his sentinel post, watching and waiting.

Inside, Doug was saying, "I just get so angry sometimes. I can't seem to control it."

"You could learn to control it."

"My anger's gotten me into trouble before, but never *this* much," Doug muttered with a look at the police cars still gathered on the street outside.

"You let everyone else go," Marnie reminded him. "If you were to decide to hand the briefcase over to the police, I'm sure they'd take that into consideration."

"You mean surrendering."

Marnie returned his glare with a challenging look of her own. "No, I mean *not* surrendering . . . to anger. I mean giving yourself a chance at life."

"You sound like you actually care," Doug noted in surprise.

"I don't like to see anyone hurting," Marnie answered.

Doug shot a worried glance out the window. Night had long since fallen, "If I show any weakness, the cops will storm the place."

"Not when you've got a bomb and me as a hostage," Marnie pointed out with soothing logic.

"All right, I'll talk to that cop," Doug relented. "But that's all, just talk."

Doug spent an hour on the phone, talking to the police negotiator who'd been called in. Marnie sat perfectly still the entire time, knowing that any distraction could well undermine Doug's shaky concentration.

Eight hours after Doug Parker had first walked into the Safe Place, he walked out again, this time with Marnie in front of him.

"Hey, they're coming out!" someone muttered.

"All right, I don't want anyone making a move until I tell them," Lieutenant Rierdon ordered.

The unarmed police negotiator walked forward and met Marnie and Doug on the steps. "You can go now, Dr. Lathrope. We'll take care of it from here."

Marnie continued down the sidewalk to the street where crowds of people were gathered. But Marnie only had eyes for one person—Logan. She headed for him with a desperation born of fear; fear that she'd never see him again, never hold him again. But here he was, waiting for her.

The last few steps between them were taken at a run as Marnie threw herself into Logan's waiting arms—arms that enclosed her with protective strength, arms that gave silent testimony to an almost palpable relief. Their embrace was fraught with emotion as they clung fiercely to each other only to draw away, as if needing the visual reassurance of seeing each other's face before truly believing the nightmare was at an end.

Within seconds Logan and Marnie were surrounded by glaring lights and electronic gadgetry. Mini–tape recorders were stuck in Marnie's face as reporters clamored to get her story. The faces whirled around her, and the voices were a meaningless babble.

Marnie blinked hard to keep a roaring darkness at bay. It didn't seem to help. The black fog rolled in, shrouding everything from view. "I'm sorry, but I believe I'm going to faint," she whispered. Having said the words, she proceeded to fulfill her prophecy.

CHAPTER TEN

Logan swept Marnie up into his arms and strode through the crowd, which parted for him as miraculously as the Red Sea did for Moses. The video cameras were all rolling, recording the anguish and concern on Logan's face as he looked down at the woman he loved. It was a look that brought many a lump to viewers' throats that night when they saw the tape on the nightly news.

When Marnie regained consciousness, she found herself draped across Logan's lap in the back of a police squad car that was definitely exceeding the legal speed limit. She felt Logan's lean fingers tremble as he ran them through her fiery hair with soothing tenderness. His husky voice poured out his love into her bemused ears. Cradled against him as she was, Marnie felt protected and safe. With a soft sigh she nestled closer to him.

But when she heard the word *hospital* being spoken, she knew she had to emerge from the beckoning cocoon. Opening her eyes, she murmured, "I don't need to go to a hospital. I'm fine."

"I know you are." His voice was husky. "I just want a second opinion, that's all. You did faint."

"I didn't eat anything all day." Marnie spoke haltingly, through teeth that seemed determined to chatter. It appeared that the echoes of violence and fear, so firmly silenced while she'd been held hostage, were now resounding through her. Tremors soon racked her body, and tears filled her brown eyes.

Logan held her and rocked her against him, absorbing her pain as if it were his own. Words fell from her lips—the random outpouring of words that comes from overwhelming stress. "I was so scared . . . I got the kids out first. . . . Carolyn was terrified. . . . I just kept talking . . . kept talking. . . . He said he had a bomb. . . ."

"I know, I know," Logan said in a soothing voice. "It's all over now. I've got you. You're safe."

"I'm sor . . . ry to be cry . . . ing for no . . . thing."

Logan tenderly wiped the tears from her face. "It's all right, Scarlett. You've earned this."

"I don't like being a crybaby," she half sobbed.

"You're not a crybaby." He kissed the tip of her nose and smoothed her hair away from her face. "You're the bravest, smartest woman in the world!"

"I don't feel very brave right now. I feel scared."

"I don't blame you." Logan traced the tracks of her tears. "I was scared too. I thought I was going to lose you." His low voice was rough with emotion. He dropped a brief but poignant kiss on her parted lips. "But you're safe, you're here with me now."

Their arrival at the hospital was marked by the sudden silencing of the squad car's wailing siren. Although Marnie insisted that she was strong enough to walk, Logan insisted even more emphatically that he would carry her. Following the police officer, Logan took her directly into the emergency room and set her onto a metal examining table. He stayed with her, holding her hand, until a harried intern came in. Even then Logan breathed down the physician's neck, barraging him with questions.

"She's fine, Mr. McCallister," the doctor said. "Her blood pressure is a bit high still, but that's to be expected." Facing Marnie, the doctor told her, "There's a police officer waiting who'd like to take your statement, if you're feeling up to it."

"Can't this wait?" Logan growled at the officer Marnie had beckoned into the room.

"I'd really rather get it over with now," Marnie said.

"Meanwhile, if you'd do the hospital a favor, Mr. McCallister?" the physician requested. "Please tell the media people swarming about the corridors and the waiting room that the excitement's over. Dr. Lathrope is fine, so they can all go home now."

Logan looked to Marnie first.

Reading his questioning gaze, she softly spoke her assurance: "I'll be okay, Logan. You go ahead."

Logan reluctantly left Marnie. He walked through the emergency room with its maze of cubbyholes and exited into the waiting room. What awaited him there was a media circus of reporters and cameramen, all talking at once.

"Give me a chance and I'll give you a statement," Logan announced.

The din immediately settled down. "Dr. Lathrope was not injured," Logan went on to say. "She should be released soon."

"Will she be making a statement then?" one reporter demanded.

"No." Logan was adamant.

"Will you tell us about your relationship with Dr. Lathrope?" another reporter asked.

"Not at this time, no." Hoping to prompt their exodus, Logan suggested, "If you guys hurry, you can make it back to your stations in time for the eleven-o'clock news."

"There's no hurry," Charlene Dawson, a female reporter from Charleston's most chatty news station, told him. "We'll be doing a live remote from right here."

Logan was not pleased to hear that. "You're wasting your time and the station's money. The story's over."

"Far from it," she drawled. "The audience loves a romantic rescue."

"On the late movie, perhaps," Logan retorted with deceptive good humor. "The news element of this story has already been covered."

Charlene made the mistake of pushing the point. "The public has a right to know, Logan. You can't allow your personal feelings to cloud the issue. Dr. Lathrope's the only one who can tell us what went on in that shelter during the eight hours she was held hostage. Did Doug Parker strike or sexually abuse her in any way?"

Logan's face paled, his eyes brilliant with anger. "No, he did not. You know, Charlene, you're a real vulture!" His inflection was gritty.

"I'm not asking any questions that you wouldn't have asked if our positions were reversed," Charlene replied.

The anchorwoman's words stayed in Logan's mind as he returned to Marnie. Had he ever pressed too hard in his quest to get to the truth? Had he indifferently stepped on people's feelings to get a good story? Disquietingly a few such occasions did come to mind. But being on the other side of the mike for a change was an enlightening experience that would end up changing the way Logan approached interviewing.

The moment he saw Marnie, Logan's frowning expression changed to a smile. "Well, Dr. Lathrope, are you just about ready to blow this joint?"

Marnie surprised him by shaking her head.

Logan immediately strode to her side. "What is it, Scarlett?"

"Nerves," she admitted with some reluctance. "You'd

think I'd feel better after what the police told me."

"Oh? What'd they say?"

"Apparently Doug was bluffing when he said he had a bomb in that briefcase. You'd think that would make me feel better."

"But it doesn't, hmm?"

She shook her head.

"Not quite ready to face the world yet?" he questioned tenderly.

"Not yet," she admitted with a shaky smile of gratitude for his perception.

"Then I'll just have to whisk you away to some place quiet and private. I know just the place too."

Logan made the arrangements with a few phone calls. Within an hour Joe had driven Logan's Datsun from the Safe Place, where he'd left it, to a side entrance of the hospital. As requested, a canvas bag stashed in the hatchback held a shaving kit and a change of clothing which Joe had picked up for Logan from the beach house.

"Thanks, buddy. I owe you one," Logan said with heartfelt sincerity.

Embarrassed by Logan's gratitude, Joe joshed, "Hey, what can I say? I guess I'm just a romantic at heart. You'd just better stay out of Eliot's way for a few days. Our exalted news director was not pleased that you didn't file a report."

"You shot enough film to keep him happy. I'll explain everything to Eliot . . . tomorrow." Logan snitched the blanket from the backseat and requested, "Meanwhile, keep an eye out for our fellow members of the press while I go get Marnie, okay?"

"Sure."

Logan returned moments later with his right arm protectively around Marnie. The blanket hung shawl-like from her shoulders as an extra protective layer between her and the chilly night air.

Joe wished them both luck as they headed off in the 280Z.

"Where are we going?" Marnie asked as Logan headed toward the Battery.

"Elaine's packed a bag for you and we'll pick it up from your place."

Not only was Elaine waiting at Marnie's place, so were Rand and her brother, Ben.

Each member of her welcoming party hugged Marnie and murmured their relief at seeing her safe and well.

Elaine wiped away tears while Rand cracked some sort of joke to ease the tension.

"Hey, kiddo, I'm glad you're okay," Ben whispered. Releasing her from his fraternal bear hug, Ben turned to speak to Logan. "The folks asked me to thank you for keeping them up-to-date during this whole thing."

"I hope to be able to meet them under more auspicious circumstances," Logan replied, noting the family resemblance between brother and sister.

"They've invited you and Marnie down to Kiawah for the holidays; sooner if you can make it."

"Thank them for me, would you? We'll be in touch real soon. Right now I think Marnie needs a little peace and quiet to recover," Logan said, nodding at the constantly ringing phone.

"Sure thing," Ben agreed.

Elaine spoke up. "Your bag's right here. And, Marnie, don't worry about your appointments on Monday. I'll see that they're all rescheduled."

"Thanks, Elaine." Marnie's words may have been softly spoken but they were from the heart.

"I'm just so glad you're safe." Elaine hugged her before

shooing them both off. "Go on, you two."

Logan could tell just how exhausted Marnie was by her lack of curiosity about their ultimate destination. She appeared content to sit in the passenger's seat with her eyes closed. Logan seemed to be taking a random course through Charleston's historic district. Actually his zigzagging through a profusion of left and right turns was intended to lose any tails that might be following them.

The Low-Country Inn, which was only a few blocks from Marnie's home, had an ambience all its own. A brick wall surrounded the property, enclosing a wisteria-draped garden. The owner, a friend of Logan's, had his best rooms ready for special guests.

Stepping into the Blue Suite was like stepping back in time. The furnishings and decorations were all authentic to the early 1800s. Even the lighting was muted in an attempt to duplicate the glow of candlelight.

But Logan's eyes weren't on the splendid furnishings, the late-covered canopied bed, or the private, fully stocked bar. Instead his gaze was fixed on Marnie's face.

"It's lovely," she said, her tired voice reflecting wistful wonder.

"I thought, with your love of antiques, that the place might appeal to you."

"It does, thank you." She squeezed his hand. "I couldn't face staying at home tonight."

"Then it's settled, Scarlett. As soon as you rid yourself of those twentieth-century trappings, I'll tuck you into this eighteenth-century bed."

"I'll change in the bathroom," she murmured.

Marnie stripped off her black jeans and oversize maroon knit sweater with a grimace. After today she wasn't sure she ever wanted to see either article of clothing again. Opening the bag Elaine had packed for her, she was pleased to see the pink batiste nightgown that she'd purchased at the flea market on the way to Myrtle Beach.

A soothing shower and shampoo helped restore some semblance of peacefulness to Marnie's soul, although they did use up her last reserves of energy. She brushed her teeth but couldn't find the strength to blow-dry her hair. Instead she wrapped it turban-style in a thick towel.

During her absence Logan had lit a cozy fire in a corner fireplace that was half hidden by a pair of wing chairs. The smell of burning hickory logs blended with the fragrant scent of a pine potpourri. Adding to the Christmasy atmosphere was a merry seasonal wreath, made entirely of pine cones, hanging safely above the mantelpiece.

Seeing that her hair was still wet, Logan drew Marnie closer to the warmth of the fire. He positioned her on a sturdy footstool before gently tugging the towel from her head and separating the damp strands of her hair with his fingers. Marnie closed her eyes in contentment as with a soothing touch he massaged her scalp, easing away the beginnings of a tension headache.

"Mmm, that feels good," she murmured, rubbing her head against his healing hand.

"You feel good," he murmured in return, adding a loving stroke to the side of her throat.

Logan continued his tender ministrations until her hair had dried. The colorful strands held a fire all their own as they curled around the tips of her shoulders with appealing abandon. Logan had never seen Marnie look more desirable, but he'd also never seen her look more exhausted. Even now her eyelids were drooping drowsily, and the smudged shadows beneath her eyes attested her need for sleep.

She was already half asleep when Logan scooped her up in

his arms and carried her over to the bed. Instead of joining her immediately, he tugged one of the blue brocade chairs over to the side of the bed and sank into it. He kept a reassuring hold on Marnie's hand, his thumb soothing the backs of her fingers with a gossamer caress as she drifted off to sleep.

How long he sat there, just looking at her face, Logan had no idea. The fire had long since died out before he quietly stripped and joined her beneath the covers. Careful not to awaken her, he eased her into his arms and held her through the night.

And so it was that he felt the first signs of her restlessness as her head shifted on the pillow and her arms thrashed about. Her muffled moans abruptly turned into a cry. "No! Don't!" Jerking awake, she jackknifed into a sitting position, tears streaming down her face.

"It's okay, I'm right here." Logan's voice soothed her as he leaned forward to gather her in his arms. "It was just a dream. It's all over now."

She huddled against him like a lost child.

His hands ran over her with tender assurance as he rested his lips upon her temple. "It's okay. I've got you now. You're safe." He said the words over and over again until, like some incantatory balm, they erased the lingering horror of her dream.

"I'm sorry." Her voice was husky.

"Do you feel like going back to sleep now?"

She shook her head without lifting it from its resting place upon his shoulder. "What time is it?"

Logan checked his wristwatch. "Three thirty."

Taking a deep breath, she sat up, away from him. "Can we talk?"

"Now?"

She nodded.

171

"Okay." He switched on a light. "Do you want to talk about your dream?"

"No, I want to talk about us."

He viewed her tear-streaked face with concern. "Marnie, I don't think this is the time—"

She put her hand to his lips. "No, let me go on. You were right about the chances of my being followed to the shelter." Her hand dropped in desolation as did her inflection. "I not only put myself in danger, I also put the rest of the residents in danger. Now, thanks to me, everyone who owns a TV set in Charleston knows where the shelter is."

"Hey!" Logan cupped her chin in his hand and directed her eyes, with their look of defeat, to the fierce pride reflected in his own eyes. "Thanks to you, all those women and their children are safe tonight. Thanks to you, Doug Parker gave himself up without hurting anyone. You saved the day, don't you know that?"

"No, I don't know that," she admitted in a choked whisper. "Right now I don't feel that I know anything."

"Do you know I love you?"

"Still?"

"Oh, Scarlett!" He pulled her back into his arms. His voice was rough with suppressed emotion as he grated, "Do you know how hard it was for me to walk out of that shelter knowing that you—the woman I love more than life itself— were still inside?" A shudder ran through him, and his arms tightened around her. "I wanted to grind Parker into the ground and set you free. But I knew that any wrong move on my part might get you killed. The only thing that saved my sanity was remembering what you'd once told me about trusting you; that you were able to take care of yourself." He loosened his hold on her, enough to lean back and study her face. "You proved that today. No one rescued you. You saved yourself and everyone else. You proved to me that even under the most grueling circumstances, you're a professional counselor who knows what she's doing, who knows how to handle a crisis and defuse it."

Marnie's smile, which had begun very tentatively, grew to reflect the feelings in her heart. Even then she needed to kiss Logan to express some measure of how much his morale-boosting speech had helped her.

Tasting the gratitude on her lips, Logan teasingly warned, "Now don't get me wrong. I'm not saying that I ever want to live through another eight hours like I did today. I think if we worked on getting a security system installed—"

"We?" Marnie questioned.

"We're a team, aren't we?"

"Oh, yes. We are most definitely a team." She spoke huskily. "Logan, I love you very much. My heart stopped when you came in and talked to Doug. I was so afraid for you. The thought of living without you terrified me ten times more than anything Doug did. I couldn't bear losing you."

"You're never going to lose me." The look in his eyes was an unspoken pledge that was reaffirmed by his impassioned kiss. "I've told you before, we were meant to be."

"Mmm." She moved against him with sensual ease. "Meant to be in bed together with a roaring fire . . ."

"I let the fire burn out a few hours ago," Logan admitted somewhat apologetically.

"Really?" Marnie propped herself up on his chest. "Then we'll just have to rekindle it, won't we?"

"Good idea," Logan murmured. One arm hooked around her, pressing her thinly clad form to his completely unclad body. With his free hand Logan guided her face down to his. Not only did he kiss her inviting lips, but he also rained gossamer-soft kisses across her entire face, proceeding at a leisurely rate that was sure to inspire delight.

Since Marnie was also showering kisses upon Logan's face, it was inevitable that their mouths crossed paths. Upon those occasions their lips merged with devotion and ardor.

When Logan spoke, Marnie could feel the words. "I never knew it was possible to miss a person as much as I missed you."

Marnie's right hand slid up the column of his throat to trace the thrust of his jaw. "I missed you just as much."

"Kissing you . . ." His lips brushed against hers. "Touching you . . ." His thumb circled the curve of her cheek. "Looking into your eyes . . ." His gaze held hers. "Those were all things I thought I'd never share with you again. I thought a glimpse of paradise was all I was going to be allowed."

Her hand shifted to soothe the sudden lines of pain from his face. "I know. But we're together again. And together we make our own paradise." Her index finger strayed from the slight stubble on his cheek, to his full lower lip. There her nail raked a delicate path across the moist fleshy skin to the outside corner of his mouth.

Expressing his pleasure with a hungry growl, Logan first rewarded her with a nibble from his strong white teeth. When she teasingly removed her finger, he then proceeded to resume the trail of kisses, leaving no portion of her face unexplored. His caressing fingers traced the curve of her jaw, from her stubborn chin up to her ear where they were greeted with unexpected receptiveness.

Marnie shivered at the simplest touch to the heretofore undiscovered erogenous zone. The curves and hollows of her ear's outer rim were tantalizingly grazed by a skillful fingertip while another fingertip descended to the spot below her ear and swirled through her hair to deliver its rhythmic beat. A moment later his tongue dipped inside the concave shell to

174

add its own special brand of seduction.

Marnie's nerve endings were alive with pleasure as she and Logan traded caresses that progressed slowly, inexorably toward intimacy. His nuzzling attention shifted from her earlobe, down to her creamy throat, where he paid special attention to the maddening throb of her pulse before moving on.

Upon reaching the neckline of her nightgown, Logan consummately set to work on the pink-ribboned lacing, eventually parting the sheer batiste material. By the time he pressed his lips to her breasts, his hands had already prepared them for his arrival. The coaxing rotation of his palms and the mounting teasing of his fingers had transformed the budding peaks into excited crests that now eagerly awaited the magic strokes of his tongue. When he touched her, she was alight with pleasure, and when he brought the tip of her breast into his mouth, she burned with a molten fire.

As she arched against him, Logan's hands slowly inched up the hem of her nightgown until it cleared her hips. A smooth half roll brought them side by side. Marnie's bent knee came to rest atop his lean hip as he submerged his powerful hardness in her welcoming softness.

"Oh, Scarlett." He groaned as she sheathed him in her exquisite embrace.

No more words were spoken as pleasure resonated between them in an electrifying current. Marnie matched his thrusts with rocking undulations. Her fluid grace conspired to lengthen the towering excitement, expanding that apex of passion into a stunning *tour de force*.

Silence continued to reign as they slowly drifted along in a hazy afterglow. Marnie was the first to speak, and when she did, her question surprised Logan. "Would you like to hear my New Year's resolution?"

His lazy drawl actually had that special cadence of

Charleston speech as he said, "Scarlett, it's not even Christmas yet."

"That doesn't matter." Her hands skimmed his waist. "Are you interested or not?"

"Definitely interested." His drawl became more sexy than lazy.

Having gained his attention, Marnie stilled her teasing fingers. "Okay, then, my resolution is to become your wife."

"Why, Dr. Lathrope, are you propositioning me?" He even batted his eyelashes at her.

"I guess I am," she acknowledged ruefully. "What do you say?"

"I think I'd rather show you my reply." And so he did in a manner that was infinitely pleasurable.

EPILOGUE

Saturday, May 10 of the next year, 7:30 P.M. (EST)

"We're going to be late!" Marnie warned her husband of four months.

"Tie this damn thing, will you?" Logan requested in a cross between a growl and a southern drawl.

Marnie took the black tie in her capable fingers and moments later charmed the stubborn tie into a perfect bow. Resting her hands on the front of Logan's dress shirt, she asked, "Have I told you how sexy you look in a tux?"

"I believe you did mention something along those lines at our wedding," he murmured, his arms encircling her waist.

"We can't be late," she warned him as he dropped a kiss to the tip of her ear.

"Of course not," he agreed, continuing his nuzzling caresses.

"This is our first fund-raiser since we relocated the shelter five months ago."

"I know." His words were muffled against her throat, where the braided strands of the garnet necklace he'd given her in Saint Martin rested against skin that was remarkable for its pearly creaminess.

"We're celebrating—"

"Feels like it to me," he inserted with a flick of his tongue.

"—the move."

Logan added a few moves of his own.

Her breathing was uneven as she said, with a half gasp, "It's a safe building."

He rocked her against him. "Very safe."

"No more roving shelters, now that we've been given this apartment building."

"No more roving," Logan repeated, his hands themselves roving over her curves.

"We were very lucky that such a wealthy benefactress decided to donate her late husband's property to us." In fact, the shelter's wealthy benefactress had once been a victim of wife beating herself. "We were very lucky," Marnie repeated in a low purring voice as Logan's caresses homed in on the crest of her breast.

"We're very lucky." Logan smiled down at his wife's passion-flushed face. "And we're also very late."

"Since we're already late, I guess there's no point in hurrying, is there?" She expertly undid the bow tie she'd just fastened.

"I love you, wife," Logan murmured.

"I love you, husband," Marnie returned.